Father By Blood

Also by Louella Bryant:

The Black Bonnet

Father By Blood

Louella Bryant

The New England Press, Inc.
Shelburne, Vermont

For HR

Manufactured in the United States of America
First Edition
Cover illustration by Gershom Griffith

For additional copies of this book or a catalog of our other titles, please write:

New England Press
P.O. Box 575
Shelburne, VT 05482

or e-mail: nep@together.net

Visit us on the Web at www.nepress.com

Bryant, Louella, 1947-
    Father by blood / Louella Bryant. -- 1st ed.
        p.   cm.
    Summary: Although fifteen-year-old Annie Brown becomes drawn into her father's battle against slavery and his raid on Harpers Ferry, she later questions both his motives and his means.
    ISBN 1-881535-33-9
    1. Harpers Ferry (W. Va.)--History--John Brown's Raid, 1859
Juvenile fiction. 2. Brown, John, 1800-1859 Juvenile fiction.
[1. Harpers Ferry (W. Va.)--History--John Brown's Raid, 1859
Fiction. 2. Brown, John, 1800-1859 Fiction. 3. Abolitionists
Fiction. 4. Fathers and daughters Fiction.]   I. Title.
PZ7.B8395Fat   1999
[Fic]--dc21
                                                                99-10953
                                                                    CIP

Contents

Author's Note

On many summer Sundays when I was growing up in northern Virginia, my mother packed a picnic lunch of fried chicken, potato salad, and a jug of lemonade, and our family loaded into the car for the two-hour drive to Harpers Ferry, West Virginia. Beneath the cliff where the enginehouse stood, we spread out lunch on a picnic table along the Shenandoah River, watched swimmers shoot the rapids in inner tubes, and listened to my father tell the story of John Brown's attempt to seize the U.S. Armory. I don't remember my father painting John Brown as a hero, but neither was he a criminal. I understood, though, that the battle at Harpers Ferry changed the course of American history forever.

In school I learned a little more about John Brown and his fight to have Kansas accepted into the Union as a free state. When his famous raid occurred, Harpers Ferry was part of Virginia, and West Virginia wasn't admitted to the Union as a separate state until 1863. Almost exactly a year after the raid, South Carolina seceded from the Union, and six months after that southern troops fired on Fort Sumter. The Civil War had begun.

It wasn't until I moved to northern Vermont that I discovered John Brown's body lies "amoulderin' in the grave" just across Lake Champlain from where I live. The Adirondack mountains were the only place where he felt at peace, and his home in North Elba, New York, just outside Lake Placid, was where he wanted to be buried.

Years after I visited Harpers Ferry with my family, I stood in front of John Brown's rustic house, which he called "Timbucto," and looked down at the grassy grave where his body rests alongside the remains of his sons and the other conspirators of the infamous raid. A great gray rock rose from the ground behind me, and to the north Whiteface Mountain stood majestic and silent. I could almost hear Annie's ax chopping up kindling, and on the wind voices singing "Blow ye the trumpet, blow."

Acknowledgments

In writing this book, I thank the following people for their help: Ed Cotter, Jan Fraga, Ron Van Ness, Richard Kuerth, Don and Monte Vanness, Linda Benoit, Sherry Gray, Spencer Smith, and Greg Wells. Two fine biographies of John Brown proved to be extremely valuable resources for my research: *Fiery Vision: The Life and Death of John Brown* by Clinton Cox and *To Purge this Land with Blood: Biography of John Brown* by Stephen Oates.

I'm especially grateful to Mark Wanner, a patient and thorough editor, and to Harry, as always, for being there.

North Elba Region

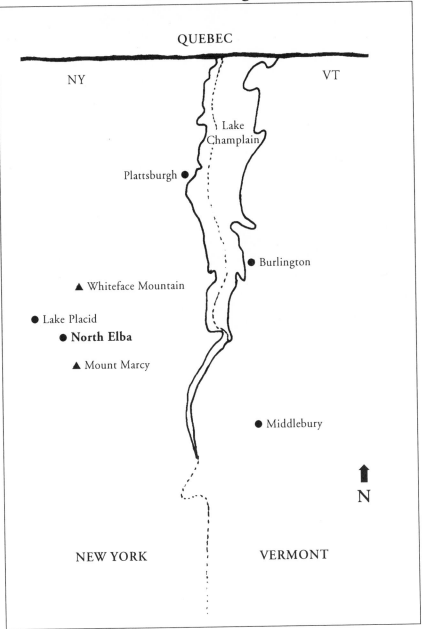

QUEBEC

NY

VT

Lake
Champlain

Plattsburgh ●

● Burlington

▲ Whiteface Mountain

● Lake Placid
● **North Elba**

▲ Mount Marcy

● Middlebury

N

NEW YORK

VERMONT

Harpers Ferry

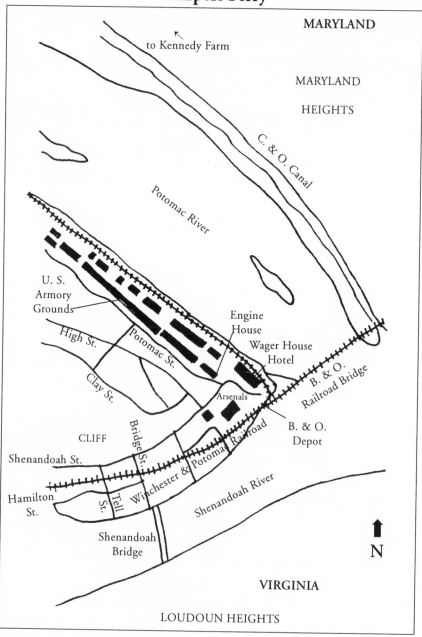

Prologue

An old woman struggled up the narrow stairway to the attic of her California home. At every other step she leaned her shoulder against the wall and rested.

In the attic, early morning light from the window outlined boxes, broken chairs, old trunks. She found her way to one special trunk and rubbed her hand over the top, brushing away years of dust. It had not been opened since she moved it from New York after her father died, more than sixty years earlier.

The latch was stubborn, but her gnarled hands were still strong, and she pried the lid open. It smelled musty, like withered flowers. She pulled out a moth-eaten shawl, a faded quilt, lace doilies, and something soft and limp. It was a pillow, its cover threadbare and sewn with a sloppy running stitch. The seam had broken open on one corner, and goose feathers puffed out. The old lady tucked them back in with a crooked finger and pressed the fabric together. She held the pillow to her face and breathed in. It smelled of sweet hay, of autumn—of Dauphin. Years after he died she finally married, but she still thought of Dauphin, his golden hair, his sparkling eyes. He was so young then, but so was she. If only things had turned out differently.

She laid the pillow aside and reached her hand into the trunk again. Cold, hard steel. She lifted the heavy object and brought it up to the light. It was a rusty pistol, a cap and ball, the kind they used before the Civil War. She ran her fingertips over the cylinder and felt the tiny cuts of an etching. Her old eyes could not see such fine detail, but she knew what it was—a navy ship, slicing through the frothy water under full sail. Her father had given her the pistol. It was still loaded with lead balls.

Resting the gun on the pillow, she felt for one more item in the bottom of the trunk. It was there, against the back, a thin, square book. She took the little volume to the window and sat on a rickety chair where she could see to read. The blue cover was worn, but she could still make out the title: *Romeo and Juliet*, by William Shakespeare. Inside was written, "To Annie on her fifteenth birthday. With all my love, your brother Oliver."

She squeezed her eyes shut, telling herself there was no use crying over what was past. And so much had passed. She saw again the huge outcropping of rock in front of the log house in North Elba, and by the huge stone, a gray monument stood with the name John Brown carved on it.

The book fell open to a page near the beginning, where she found Romeo's words:

O me! what fray was here?
Yet tell me not, for I have heard it all,
Here's much to do with hate but more with love . . .
Feather of lead, bright smoke, cold fire, sick health,
Still-waking sleep that is not what it is—

Had it been a dream—the hiding, the fighting, the dying? She was the only child of John Brown left alive; there was no one to help her remember. Some said her father was a villain who led the country into civil war. Others said he was a hero who helped free the slaves. Even after all these years, she wasn't sure she really knew the man called rebel, assassin, man of God, Osawatomie Brown—the man she called Father.

Was he a good man? Would a good man have taken his men into hopeless battle? Would a good man have led his own sons to their deaths? People said John Brown's raid on Harpers Ferry started the Civil War. She didn't blame him for wanting to end slavery. But could she ever forgive him for tearing apart her family?

Now that her life was drawing to an end, she wanted to make peace with her memories. She wanted to look back, back across the country, back across time to the year 1859. Maybe at last she could make peace with John Brown.

Chapter 1

Martha was kneeling at the feet of the dark-skinned man sitting on a kitchen chair. From the pot on the stove I'd ladled warm water into a pan, and she was washing his cut-up feet with a clean cloth and wrapping the wounds with bandages. Cyrus had walked a long way through brambles and brush to get this far north and, although he didn't have much farther to go to get to the border of Canada, he couldn't travel another night with raw, bleeding feet. He'd have to rest a few days at Timbucto. As long as he was here, we'd have to keep a look-out for strangers. Anyone not from North Elba might be a slave catcher.

The kettle was coming to a boil. I set out three cups for tea while Martha finished with Cyrus. Martha had become part of our family since she married my brother Oliver. She was just a year older than I, and we had come to be the best of friends. She was a big help with the chores, especially the cooking and mending, which I tried to avoid.

As I was about to fill the cups, someone banged on the front door.

"Root cellar," I said, pointing to a narrow opening off the kitchen. Martha pushed Cyrus toward the dark hole where we kept potatoes, turnips, and parsnips. It would be the first place the bounty hunters would look unless we could throw them off, but there was no time for a better idea.

Martha picked up the bandaging and set the chair against the wall while I went to the door. It was made of thick oak and opened with a heavy creak.

Dauphin Thompson stood on the stoop, his blond curls blown around his broad face. Dauphin wasn't bad looking, and he was closer to my age than any other male in North Elba. His brother married my sister Ruth, and my brother Watson was married to his sister, and I expected when it came time, he and I would marry, too. Dauphin must have considered me as a prospect. Why else did he come to visit nearly every day? But he knew better than to use the front door, which was reserved for Sunday visitors. The only others who came to the front were strangers—and slave catchers. And with a fugitive in the kitchen, I was edgy.

Dauphin's blue eyes flicked about quickly, up the road, over my shoulder, onto my face.

"He's coming," he said, out of breath.

"Who's coming?" I snapped back. I didn't have time for guessing games.

"Bounty hunter. Same one I saw snooping around here last week. Better hide that fugitive and I'll try to head him off."

"It won't do any good," I said, pulling him inside so I could shut the door behind him. "They always come here first. If anyone's hiding a fugitive, it's John Brown's family,

5

and they know it."

"You want me to find a place in the barn?" Dauphin asked.

"No," I said. "Just meet him and try to slow him down." I looked around, trying to think. Steam was rising from the kettle, and the wire pot handle fell over and clanked against the metal as if trying to get my attention.

"Then what?" asked Dauphin.

"Bring him around the south side of the house." Dauphin looked confused. "The side with the upstairs windows." I tried to make it clear to him. "I'll do the rest."

Dauphin bolted out the door, and I latched it after him.

"Stay put," I yelled into the root cellar. Then I grabbed the cloth Martha was using to wipe Cyrus' feet and wrapped it around the pot handle.

"Get the kettle," I ordered Martha. "We'll need all the hot water we can haul." I struggled up the narrow stairs, my wool skirt wicking up the water I sloshed out, and Martha followed close behind with the kettle.

The second floor of our log cabin was an open space. Quilts hanging from ropes divided it into smaller rooms for my married brothers and my younger sisters and me. Mother and Father slept downstairs in a small room off the kitchen.

Light poured in through the tall paned windows at the southern end, and I slid up a lower section and heaved the pot up to rest on the sill. Martha poured the scalding water from the kettle to fill the pot to the brim. A fresh breeze wafted in. We'd had a hard frost the middle of May, and it was still cool now at the beginning of June. I trusted the water would stay hot long enough to do its job.

We waited. I was glad Mother was in town with my

sisters. She was never too happy with me. She thought now that I was fifteen, it was time I started acting like a lady. I imagined Mother wouldn't take too kindly to what I was about to do.

A horse whinnied, and Martha and I stood on each side of the pot and gripped the handle with the cloth to keep from burning our hands.

Dauphin's voice said, "Maybe he's in the barn around back. This way."

A black fly buzzed and footsteps rustled the tall grass. I hoped and prayed Dauphin had the sense to get out of the way.

I saw Dauphin's yellow curls first. He shot a quick glance toward the window and then made a wide arc away from the house. The other man was between Dauphin and the house and coming within range. Even from our high post I could see he was squat and overfed, and his leather riding boots were dusty from the road. I couldn't see his face under the brim of his hat, but the end of his nose stuck out like he was sniffing out the scent of our illegal guest. I didn't like his looks. My fingers twitched on the pot handle.

Just as he lined up with the window, Martha and I pushed our hips against the pot, and the water cascaded down in a steamy stream right on target.

"I hope we scalded him good," I told Dauphin later.

"Aw," he said, "it wasn't no more than a hot bath."

"Where'd he go off to?" I asked.

"Said he was going into town to get some salve—and dry clothes."

"We've got to get Cyrus someplace safe before he comes back," I said.

7

Dauphin went to the barn to get Oliver and Watson. Of my six older brothers, Watson was most like a father to me. While Father was off in Kansas or Missouri fighting against slavery or down in Pennsylvania or Washington raising money for the cause, Watson stayed home to tend the farm and watch over Mother and the children. He was quiet and simple, and we depended on him.

In no time Watson had the horse hooked to the wagon, and Oliver hid Cyrus in back under feed bags and hay. Then they headed off toward the Lake Champlain ferry to Vermont, where conductors on the underground railroad would help Cyrus get to Canada. I thought about Father. He would be proud of us for saving another soul from bondage.

Chapter 2

Thinning carrots wasn't hard work. I preferred it to sweeping out the hen house, where the acrid odor of chicken droppings was strong enough to choke me. The carrot sprouts were thin and lacy, and they tickled my wrists like green feathers. The pleasant smell of ox manure hovered over the field, reminding me the earth had come to life again, bringing with it the promise of new things. For no reason at all I felt hopeful.

I stopped thinning and pressed the sleeve of my shirt to my sweating forehead. The air was cool this cloudless day, but with the bright sun and hard work, I felt hot. I had three more rows to thin before noon, but I was taking my time about it. If Father had been home, he would have pressed me to be finished by now and on to another chore.

My father was a farmer, not much different from any other farmer in North Elba. He raised sheep and kept a milking cow and a pair of oxen for pulling the plow. He went to church on Sunday. Once in a while he was called on to preach because his voice boomed from the pulpit, and he could keep the gentlemen from falling asleep. On those Sundays he always spoke out against enslavement. Most northern farmers were opposed to slavery, and a few called themselves abolitionists, but I didn't know any fathers who were as adamantly against slave holding as mine.

Oliver was chopping wood up by the house. With a clunk, his ax bit into a log and cleaved it in two. I loved all my brothers, but Oliver was my favorite. He was handsome, with eyes as blue as robins' eggs and a round face framed by dark waves of hair. When I was with him, I didn't feel the need to talk. Oliver wasn't much of a talker anyway, but he had a way of showing his feelings—a raised eyebrow meant he was considering a proposition or a twitch at the corner of his mouth showed he was pleased. Every resting minute he had his nose in a book, and not just the Bible or Puritan sermons like Father read. Oliver studied Emerson's essays on nature, and he lost himself in Shakespeare and Henry Wadsworth Longfellow's poetry. If he appreciated beauty in words, he must have appreciated it in women, too, because Martha was the prettiest girl in North Elba.

When he had stacked the split pieces of wood by the house, Oliver went to work on another log. Our cabin was not elegant. Plain and square, it reflected Father's distaste for unnecessary adornment. The exterior was of unpainted wood with two brick chimneys spouting from opposite ends of the steep roof, one for the parlor stove and the other for the cook stove in the kitchen.

The front door faced east toward Mount Marcy, New York's highest peak, and to the north a jagged mountain with a white scar stood all alone. Whiteface Mountain, craggy and rocky and still topped with snow, looked close in the crisp morning air. It must have held stories as old as the beginnings of the earth, stories about strange creatures who trudged through the valleys millions of years ago, people who hunted with clubs, early settlers and the first smoke that curled from stone chimneys toward its summit.

We moved here from Ohio, but Dauphin grew up in North Elba. His grandfather had told him tales about the big jagged mountain, and Dauphin recounted them to me. My favorite was the story of the white stag who used to roam the Adirondacks, a buck so powerful that no regular arrows could puncture the hide. One day a young brave with two magic arrows in his quiver stalked the great stag to the top of the mountain. There in the mist it stood, coat white as milk, head high, nose to the wind. It was twice the size of any buck the brave had ever seen. The young warrior fixed the first arrow on his bow, drew back the string, and let the arrow fly, piercing the stag's neck. The second arrow drove into his haunch. The brave, thinking he would give the snowy hide to the Iroquois princess he loved, tried to climb the rock to claim his prize. But, try as he could, he was not able to reach the ledge where the arrows had pinned the stag. The next day when the brave returned to try again, the stag was gone, but where it died, the rock had turned white. From that day on, the Iroquois called the mountain Whiteface.

I looked at the mountain pointing into the blue sky and tried to imagine Dauphin as the brave and me as the Iroquois princess. I wondered if he had ever thought of me that way, if he'd ever try to win a prize for me. Someday maybe he and I would climb Whiteface and see the

11

white rock close up. Maybe he would hold my hand or put his arm around my waist. Maybe . . .

"Annie!" someone called.

Lyman Epps was standing by the wood pile with Oliver and waving his straw hat at me. He was a fine-looking dark-skinned man who never paid a visit without bringing us a little something, poor as his family was.

"Mr. Epps brought us a jar of maple syrup," said Oliver.

"Thank you kindly," I said, leaving the carrots. It was always a pleasure to visit with Lyman Epps.

"Mrs. Epps sends you her regards," said Mr. Epps. He smiled and hit his thigh with his hat. "Junior's tending the farm this morning while I run some errands in town. Anyone want to come along?"

"I still have a load of chopping to do," said Oliver.

I had no money to spend, but I wanted to see the townspeople and hear the latest news. I'd never dare think of leaving my work if Father were around, but he hadn't been home for two months. The carrots could wait a little longer for thinning.

"Mr. Epps," I said, "I believe I'll join you."

Lyman Epps's family lived on the land in North Elba donated by Gerrit Smith, a wealthy businessman in Peterboro, New York. Mr. Smith set aside a hundred thousand acres for free blacks to farm. Father purchased more than two hundred acres himself and named it Timbucto, after a town in Africa. He planned to live among the blacks and help them get started, but so far only about twelve families had settled in. The woods needed clearing and the open ground was either low and swampy or filled with stones, but nobody complained. We all shared what little we had to help each other through the long, hard winters.

"You have business in town, Mr. Epps?" I asked as we walked along.

"Yes," he said, lifting the burlap bag he was carrying. "I'm hoping to sell these potatoes at the starch factory and see about a nice piece of leather at the tannery." I liked the way he spoke. He'd gone to school in Troy and had more education than I did. I'd learned enough to read and write, enough to teach my sister Sarah, who would teach baby Ellen. We'd moved so often that I hadn't had time to get much formal schooling, but I hoped to make up for it someday.

While Mr. Epps was in the starch factory, I waited outside and watched wagons roll down North Elba's main road, the horses laboring through a layer of mud. Akron, where we lived before we moved here, was a much bigger town. Main Street was lined with millinery shops, restaurants, and confectioners' stores, where the smells of vanilla and peppermint made my mouth water. Ladies wore fancy dresses, and boardwalks kept the hems of their dresses from dragging in the dirt while they shopped. On Sunday afternoons Main Street turned into a parade route of families riding through town in their go-to-meeting clothes. In North Elba no one had time for such foolishness. Farm chores had to be tended to, even on Sundays. Besides, there wasn't much downtown to brag about—a dry goods and feed store, the tannery and starch factory, and an iron foundry at the end of the road. I felt confined and restless. Even though I knew almost everyone in town, North Elba didn't appeal to me. I was waiting for my chance to leave and see the bigger world.

Mr. Epps came out of the starch factory, and we walked to the tannery. Inside, the tannery smelled of harnesses, of saddles and reins, of belts and boots and gunstraps. It was the scent of power and control, a smooth, strong smell I wanted to wrap around myself.

Two men stood talking to Harmon Wheeler, the clerk. The men must have worked at the foundry because their clothes were sooty, and their skin was stained dark gray, darker than Mr. Epps, who was the color of rich honey. The three men were laughing and seemed to be finished with their business, but Harmon ignored Mr. Epps.

"Excuse me," said Mr. Epps. "If you don't mind, I'd like to buy some leather." He held his straw hat in his hands.

Harmon looked my friend up and down. Mr. Epps stood tall with his shoulders back. His clothes were frayed with wear, but he was neat.

"We don't do business with coloreds," Harmon said. The foundry men snickered.

"I have money," said Mr. Epps.

"Maybe you didn't hear me, boy," said Harmon.

Mr. Epps crushed the brim of his hat with his big, callused hands. A muscle twitched in his cheek. "I heard you," he said.

"You want us to show him what kind of business we'll do with him?" said one foundry man, stepping close to Mr. Epps.

"May be a good idea," said Harmon, staring Mr. Epps in the eye.

I didn't like the direction the conversation was headed. Mr. Epps had done nothing wrong, and I didn't think he'd even strike back if a white man hit him.

"Mr. Wheeler," I broke in. "Remember me? I'm Annie, John Brown's daughter. And this is Lyman Epps, our friend. Maybe you didn't recognize him." I smiled as sweetly as I could, trying not to show how I was feeling.

For the past four years the newspapers had reported the details of my father's battles with the slaveowners in Kansas. He had been determined that Kansas would be admitted to the Union as a free state and had won, but not without bloodshed. I was well aware of the weight my father's name carried.

"I'm sure it would make my father happy if you'd wait on Mr. Epps," I said.

"Your father's Osawatomie Brown?" said one of the foundry men, wide-eyed.

I nodded. Father had earned the name in Osawatomie, Kansas, the site of the fiercest conflict between the slaveowners and the Free-Staters.

"Didn't mean no harm," said the man.

"We'd best get back to work," said the other man, moving toward the door. "Looks like Harmon's got a customer."

Chapter 3

Warm summer days were in short supply, and we considered them a great luxury. I had only to chop enough wood for cooking, and the livestock took care of themselves, grazing in the field and drinking from the pond. Most crops were not yet ready for harvesting, and the weeds were under control. There was time to hike through the woods with Dauphin and pick wild blackberries or sit on the big rock in front of the house and read. Precious as the leisure time was, though, it would come to an end when Father returned. He would rouse the family before daylight and see to it that every member of the household had a gainful task. Every minute away from labor was an opportunity for the devil, he'd say. It was apparent that John Brown did not intend to give the devil any chance to invade his home.

I loved Father, but I almost dreaded his return because it meant long days of hard work and longer evenings of prayers. His lectures about the downtrodden seemed endless, especially since I didn't feel at all privileged myself. My threadbare skirt barely touched the top of my boots, and the waistband was so tight I left it unfastened and covered it with a sash. There was no money for cloth, and all we had was the rough homespun Mother wove.

I knew better than to complain to Father. Although he had never whipped me, my older brothers told me they had felt the bite of a stinging branch. Brother Owen said that when he was young he earned eighteen lashes when one of the sheep wandered off from the flock he was tending. Father laid six good strokes on him. Then he stripped off his own shirt and gave the switch to Owen.

"Lay it on my back," Father told him. "And if you hold back, I'll turn the switch on you again."

Owen, in fear of disobeying his father, gave twelve hearty blows until drops of blood appeared where the tip of the branch cut through the skin.

"Remember," Father told him, "sometimes God visits His punishment upon the innocent." In those days Father did not inflict a punishment without bringing it upon himself. I wondered if he still felt that way.

Father was due home any day. It was the third of July, and if we were to have a real holiday, it had to be before his return.

At dinner I told Dauphin's story of the white stag and the brave on Whiteface Mountain.

"I've heard that story," said Oliver.

"A tall tale, if you ask me," said Salmon. He was next to Oliver in age, but he seemed much older. He had been wounded fighting in Kansas and barely escaped with his life.

"It's an Iroquois legend," said Oliver.

"Well, I'd have to see that stag to believe it," scoffed Salmon.

"Then let's hike up and see it," I offered.

Salmon looked at me. He may have been thinking what I was—there would be no hiking when Father came home.

"Father would want to know what climbing a mountain will bring to the greater good of humanity," he said.

"Must Father find out about it?" I asked.

"He seems to know things without being told," muttered Salmon. Even in his absence, Father's will imposed itself.

"Then let's just say it's an exercise to keep us fit for the work that lies ahead," I said. "And if we find ourselves having a little fun, we must promise to try not to enjoy it!"

No one laughed, but the mood at the table lightened, and I could see my brothers begin to take the idea seriously.

"Mr. Hinkley has a boat," Salmon said. He was married to Mr. Hinkley's daughter, Abbie. "We could take his wagon to Paradox Landing and row up Lake Placid to the trail head."

"When shall we go?" asked Watson.

"Tomorrow's the fourth," I volunteered. "What better way to celebrate Independence Day?"

Oliver stayed at Timbucto to help Mother with the chores, and early the next morning we set out in Mr. Hinkley's wagon for Paradox Landing, where he kept his boat. Watson's wife Belle came along, and Salmon brought his wife Abbie. I was glad Dauphin could come, since the whole idea for the trip came from his story—but I was also glad because I liked having him around.

The boat trip from Paradox took two and a half hours, according to Mr. Hinkley's watch, during which time Watson and Salmon took turns with the oars. At the foot of the trail we strapped our bedrolls on our backs, and Salmon and Watson stuffed their packs with the food we needed for two days.

The weather, warm and clear, made the hike easy going at the start. Along the path wild daisies, bunchberries, and flowering mosses grew, and brown spotted toads hopped out of the way.

When the trail grew steeper, we marched single file up the creek bed, Watson in the lead and Mr. Hinkley bringing up the rear. My long legs were strong and a match for any man's, and once I had to stop and wait for Dauphin. A few brave birds called, and black flies buzzed around my head. The tips of the evergreen boughs were yellow with new growth, and above them, rocks jutted out like the bony back of a giant lizard.

When Dauphin caught up, I pointed to a rock formation near the mountaintop. "Doesn't it look like a face?"

"That's the Indian brave," Dauphin said. He took my hand, and I felt a tingling where our palms touched. His hand was cool and dry and much softer than I expected it to be.

"If you look up toward the summit, you can just make out that white stag I told you about," he said.

I studied the mountain. He was right. I could see the outline of a stag, an immense animal, antlers and all. Could the Indian tale have had some truth to it?

Dauphin squeezed my hand before he let it go.

We hiked on, stopping to have a bite to eat and catch our breath. Finally, after four hours of climbing, we reached the top of Whiteface Mountain.

I looked out across the expanse of sky and earth. Below us was the northern end of Lake Placid, its dark blue water surrounding an island of evergreen trees. Beyond, another island sat in a still haze, and I could make out Paradox at the southern end of the lake. In the distance Mount Marcy stood tall and majestic, and nestled somewhere in the low area between the two peaks lay North Elba and Timbucto. My sisters Sarah and Ellen were too young to make the trip, but they may have been looking up at Whiteface at that very moment.

To the east, Lake Champlain was a long gray stretch of water with sailboats drifting lazily on it. A steamboat churned south, the same boat Father had taken many times on his trips to and from Timbucto. Across the lake were the Green Mountains of Vermont. I could see the one they called Camels Hump, but it looked more like a lion, head up, watching its prey. Farther east lay New Hampshire.

Mr. Hinkley took out a handkerchief and wiped the sweat from his neck. He was nothing like Father. First of all, I couldn't imagine Father hiking up a mountain for no good reason other than to see the view from the top. Everything Father did had to have a goal at the end of it, whether it was farming or business or abolition. Mr. Hinkley was large and soft; Father was all bone and muscle. Mr. Hinkley had an agreeable manner, and grace and good humor surrounded him. Father was strict and stern, and the few times I saw him laugh, his body quaked faintly, like a spasm, but not a sound came from his mouth.

"To your left," said Mr. Hinkley, "you can see the Sentinel Range."

"Father takes the route through those mountains sometimes," said Salmon. "There's a narrow dirt road that

20

passes between the Sentinels and the Cascades. He goes on foot so he won't be seen."

Ever since the upheaval in Kansas, Father had to be careful about his anti-slavery activities. He'd made more enemies than friends, and slavery advocates watched for any reason to have him locked away. But he still managed to travel all over the country. He took his sons to fight with him in Kansas, all except Watson. I'd lived in North Elba for four years now, and it seemed like forever. I dreamed of seeing far-away places and walking the dirt roads with Father. I was sure he wouldn't be an easy companion, but my longing to leave North Elba was stronger than my apprehensions about Father.

"Up north," Mr. Hinkley said, "you can see Canada." Canada. The slaves called it the promised land, and they gambled their lives to get there. It seemed so close now, I felt like I could reach out and touch it.

Dauphin was standing behind me and I could feel his breath on my hair. He smelled of sweet hay. "Beautiful," he whispered. I knew he meant the view, but I wished he was talking about me.

That night I bedded down on a mattress of soft moss. There were no trees on the mountaintop to block the view, and when I looked up at the still, silent night, I felt free—free of the earth, free of gravity, free from the boredom of my daily chores at Timbucto.

Then I saw, clear as the stars in the cloudless sky, a dark-skinned girl my own age lying on her cot and looking out through the window of her quarters, her eye on the north star just as mine was, and following the dipper of the drinking gourd as it points north. I couldn't move. Pain flowed through my body, and to my astonishment, I realized that I was feeling her aching muscles, the gnawing hunger in her stomach, the stinging wounds where the lash bit into her skin. But mostly I felt sadness, her despair that all she had to look forward to was more of the punishment and pain that had been hers that day. She thought of freedom, a brief glimmer of hope in a dark night, but more, she thought of death, a blessed escape from a short life of hard work and suffering. When she shivered under her thin blanket, I shivered in my warm bedroll. I saw her burnished skin, her opal eyes and felt as my own the tear that left a silver trail across her temple. I'd never seen her before, but in an instant I knew her as if she were my own sister.

I sat up, and the girl vanished. Toads croaked in the distance, and from the bulky bedrolls of my brothers came the heavy breathing of sleep. My heart thumped a quick rhythm. I had not been dreaming; I hadn't even been asleep. The vision was more powerful, more disturbing, more real than any dream. I tried to breathe deeply, slowly, to calm my heart and stop the trembling in my muscles. What did it mean? I knew the evils of slavery—any child of John Brown had to—but, except for helping the fugitives who found their way to our door, I hadn't done anything to help Father's cause. Was this vision telling me now was the time?

I lay back down, but I tossed and tumbled a long time that night until the words of Father's favorite hymn floated through my mind. It was a hymn he'd sung to my brothers and to me, and he still sang it to the younger girls.

Blow ye the trumpet, blow
The gladly solemn sound;
Let all the nations know

To earth's remotest bound,
The year of Jubilee is come,
Return, ye ransomed sinners home!

Just as I drifted off to sleep, I was sure I heard, ever so faintly, a sound like the braying of a great stag, a trumpet note sweet and clear on the night air, calling to me.

Chapter 4

"How long will you be home this time, Father?" I asked.

I couldn't get used to seeing my father with a white beard, especially one that reached his chest. It hid the hard set of his mouth and gave him an old and haggard appearance. His hair had grown long and wild, and if I hadn't known who he was, I might have thought him a madman.

"Long enough to reacquaint myself with my family and check my sheep." Father always spoke in metaphors. His family were his children, and by sheep he meant his army, which were to some measure the same, since six of his sons had fought with him in Kansas. As for his family at Timbucto, little Ellen now toddled about the house, Sarah was the age I had been when we moved to North Elba, and with Belle, Abbie, and Martha, three more women's hands had been added to help stir the pot.

When Father came home, we expected the house to spring to life—he would find fences to mend, harnesses to repair, roofs to patch, and put everyone to work tending to details his children neglected while he was gone. But the first morning after his arrival, he stayed in bed with a fever. At first my concern was mingled with relief, but by midday, when he had not risen, I began to feel alarm. Maybe the abolition work was weighing on him. I sat with him while his fever persisted, wiping his brow with a cool cloth.

"My strange Anna," he murmured. At least he was well enough to remember his pet name for me, although I was never sure why he thought me strange. Maybe it was the way I looked—I wasn't nearly as pretty as my sisters. More likely it was because I preferred to help Watson drive the oxen across the field than to sit inside and sew. Even in Akron, my childhood playmates were mostly boys, and I would have worn trousers if Mother hadn't put her foot down against it.

"A long time ago," he struggled to say.

"Hush, Father," I urged. "You must rest." But he kept talking.

"When I was younger than you are now, I used to help my father round up wild steer. We drove them all the way from Ohio to the Michigan Territory so the soldiers in the outposts would have meat on their plates. It was a distance of some hundred miles. We got to know folks along the way, and they fed us supper and gave us a place to sleep for the night."

He took a drink of water. The fever and talking had made his mouth dry. I had a feeling that once he got his story out, he'd feel better.

"My father's tannery got so busy that he allowed me to drive the cattle by myself. One night I stayed at the house of a gentleman landlord who owned a slave boy about the same age I was. At dinner the gentleman and some other men at the table made a fuss over how well spoken I was and how well mannered, how good I was to be so far from home and handling a herd of cattle alone. And then the slave boy came in to clear away the plates. I was wearing fine boots and a leather belt, and all he had were ragged britches and a sullied shirt, and no shoes at all. He was all skin and bones, as if he'd eaten nothing but leavings from his master's table. He was looking at me so hard that he dropped one of the glasses, and it shattered on the floor. The landlord was irked with the boy and grabbed an iron shovel from the fireplace. He commenced to beat him around the head and shoulders so that the poor wretch had to shield himself with his arms."

He raised up on one elbow. The color came back to his sunken cheeks and fire flashed in his eyes, and I felt a shiver of apprehension. This was the old Father, who caused his allies to revere him and his enemies to quake in fear.

"I shall never forget that boy and his helpless state," he said.

As I listened to his story, I began to feel dizzy. The room seemed to grow dark and my head throbbed. I couldn't move. Then slowly I could see again, but Father's bedroom had disappeared and I was in a grand room with polished wood all about. Father was there, but he was lying on a cot, bandaged about the head and chest. Two rows of seated men looked down at him, and armed guards stood on either side of his cot. One man rose, a piece of paper in his hand. On it was written one word—GUILTY.

Guilty? Of what? The polished wood, the rows of men—it must have been a jury, a courtroom. And the bandages; he had been wounded. Were the armed men protecting him from attackers or were they protecting everyone else from the frail old man who couldn't even get up from his cot? Jury trials were for serious criminals—thieves and traitors and murderers. Father loved his country. He read the Bible and raised his children by it. What could he have done to cause such a scene?

"My strange Anna," said Father. He patted my hand and lay back on the pillow.

When he touched me, the vision faded away and I was sitting in his room again, staring at his angular face. I tried to tell myself that I was imagining things, but I couldn't stop the prickling feeling on my skin that the visions were more than that. I was fearful for Father, but I couldn't let him know it. Almost as much as he detested slavery, he hated weakness, especially in his own children.

"Father," I forced myself to say, "you've made great progress with abolition."

"I feel considerable regret that I have lived so many years and have in reality done so very little to increase the amount of human happiness," he whispered.

"It's your fever talking," I protested.

"I have a sad heart," he said. "I've borne the humiliation of begging the means to feed and equip my men. I can make no further sacrifices."

I didn't believe a word of it. Father's labors had worn on him, but he didn't give up when he was outnumbered by pro-slavery armies out west, nor when he was accused of murdering slave owners. The richest men in the country put their money behind him, and his allies were people like Harriet Tubman and Frederick Douglass, the runaway slaves who were now working for abolition. Osawatomie Brown wouldn't give up now. But the vision of the courtroom was grim. I had a feeling Father's greatest challenge was still ahead of him.

I held a spoonful of chicken soup to his lips. When he had taken it, he said, "I have told your brothers, and now I will tell you." For a moment the energy seemed to surge back into him. "I'd like the old monument brought from Kansas that was carved from granite for my grandfather. I value the old relic for its age and homeliness, and it is of sufficient size to contain more inscriptions." He smiled weakly. "It will be a great curiosity." And then he closed his eyes.

For an instant I thought Father might be dying, but God wouldn't take him now when he had so much work left to do on earth. And the vision—I hoped I was wrong, but I was afraid the scene in the courtroom would be played out, for better or for worse.

When Father was asleep, I went out to where Watson was working the field with the oxen. Oliver was leading Moses and I took hold of old Ruby's yoke and walked along with them. The air was scented with rhododendron, elder blossoms, and dogtooth violets. I lifted my skirt and stumbled over the furrowed ground. At the end of the row, Watson turned the oxen and started back toward the house, and I looked across the field at the huge boulder that stuck up through the ground in front of our house. Father always said he wanted to be buried there by the big rock, but I hadn't noticed before what a long shadow it cast.

In the afternoon Lyman Epps came to see Father.

"I'm told that Mr. Brown has a fever," he said. "I thought I'd see if I could help."

When Mr. Epps sat in the chair by the bed, Father seemed to perk up.

"Mr. Epps," he said. "What a pleasure."

"I brought you some yarrow tea, Mr. Brown," he said and held up a glass jar filled with a green liquid. Cloth was tied to the top with string, and Mr. Epps removed it and handed the jar to Father. "My wife brewed it this morning. It always takes the ague right out of me."

"Why, thank you," Father said. He had never drunk tea or coffee as far as I knew, but he must have trusted Mrs. Epps' medical skill because he drank it right down.

Mr. Epps sat quietly by, and after several minutes Father said, "This lying about is worrisome."

"Well, now, Mr. Brown, I think you've earned a good rest."

"Rest is another word for sloth, my friend. I do not like to think that even Heaven is a place of rest. It must be a state of activity where all our powers are being continually developed for the better."

As Father spoke, Mr. Epps stroked his beard with one large hand. The other was on his knee.

"Mr. Epps," said Father, sitting up, "your parents were slaves, were they not?"

"Yes, they were," said Mr. Epps. "They lived on a Maryland plantation, and their master freed them when he got too old to manage the farm. That was before I was born."

"Then you know how vile and unjust slavery is. I'd like to enlist your help in putting an end to it."

"What can I do, Mr. Brown? I'm just a farmer."

"Tomorrow evening come to the house. God willing, I'll be recovered enough to gather my sheep and deliver our next plan of action."

I looked up. Father was ready for his next attack on slavery. I had never tried to listen to his plans before, but the images came back to me of the slave girl and of Father lying wounded. Tomorrow evening I would pay close attention to what happened at the meeting, because I had a feeling that Father's next plan of action was going to involve me.

"We have work to do, children," Father said the next morning. He seemed to have gained back his old strength. He directed sheep to be sheared and the wool washed, carded, and readied for spinning, the hen house was repaired, and the ox yoke inspected.

When I came from the chicken coop with eggs cradled in my skirt, I saw Father standing in front of the giant rock, his lean hands drawn into fists at his side. He stood so motionless studying the outcropping that he looked himself to be carved of stone, a weathered pillar.

"It is only a sense of duty and obligation that keeps me from laying my bones to rest here," he said. He took a deep breath.

I looked at his profile—the long, slender nose, the sharp cheekbones. I'd lost brothers and sisters to diseases and accidents. My brother Frederick was killed in Kansas, Salmon was wounded, and who knew what lay in store for all of us with Father's next plan?

"If my path leads into the valley of death," he said, "I know that God intends some good to come of it."

The wind whispered around us and then settled into silence.

Chapter 5

After supper Dauphin arrived, and he had with him his older brother Henry and my sister Ruth, Henry's wife. Lyman Epps followed them in. The men gathered in the parlor while we women dawdled in the kitchen, being quiet enough to hear what was said in the other room. I heard chairs scrape across the floor, and voices cleared before they settled down to serious talk.

"This southern course of action," said Father, "may be the momentum we need to swing the pendulum our way."

"What exactly is the course of action?" Salmon's voice.

"The original plan was to move every slave south of Maryland to Canada, but that prospect is unrealistic. Even if I had the men to lead the exodus, the funds are too slim to feed and clothe, shelter, and arm so many."

"And the number of slaves to transport." I recognized Henry's voice. "Well, it just can't be done."

"I have devised what I believe to be a more immediate

and effective alternative," Father said.

"Have you decided to let the slaves free themselves?" asked Salmon.

"In a manner of speaking. One of my wealthy allies has provided a sufficient number of rifles to set the plan in motion. The rest are waiting for us at Harpers Ferry, Virginia."

"Explain, Father." It sounded like Watson.

"Harpers Ferry is the home of the United States Armory. They have twenty workshops turning out the hardware we need—enough rifles to arm every enslaved person in the United States."

I looked at Ruth. Her wide eyes suggested she was thinking the same thing I was. Was Father planning to steal guns from the Federal government? Did he intend for slaves to shoot their way out of bondage? The idea was insane.

"What chance do you have?" Henry asked.

"If God be for us, who can be against us?" came Father's response. God was his answer for everything. Maybe God was the reason he didn't fear death. But what about his men?

"What makes him think God is on his side?" whispered Abbie. Abbie was new to our family, and she hadn't learned that John Brown's children did not question his decisions, at least not out loud.

"Are you with me?" Father asked the men.

Abbie's skirt disappeared through the threshold, and I followed after her. I wasn't going to miss this showdown, even though my blood was racing.

"Salmon is not with you, sir," she said.

Father looked at her with the gentle amusement he usually reserved for little Ellen. He had not taken her seriously.

"That decision is up to Salmon," he said.

"Salmon always considers my point of view. I am his wife, after all." Abbie planted her fists on her hips.

"And he is your husband and will make his own decisions," Father said. He looked at my brother.

"Salmon?"

Salmon sat on a wooden chair with his elbows on his knees. He stared for a moment at the floor, and then he sighed. He stood up, walked over to Abbie, and put an arm around her waist.

"You'll have to fight this one without me," he said.

I almost gasped in surprise, but I couldn't blame him. He had nearly lost an arm in Kansas, and it seemed to me that without divine intervention, the odds for coming out of Harpers Ferry whole were not good.

Father gripped the arms of his chair and locked eyes with Salmon. With his gray eyes and white beard, he looked as if a frost had gripped him, and I felt a chill run through me. When he spoke, his cold voice seemed to strike Salmon as painfully as a lash.

"I never questioned my father's requests of me," he said. "I expect the same of my own sons."

I looked at Father, and it felt like I had never seen him before. Did he really expect his sons to follow him without hesitation into such peril?

Salmon paced back and forth across the small parlor.

"When I was in Kansas, my clothes were worn to tatters and I lived for a month on only Indian meal and water. I gave all I had in Kansas except my life. I won't tempt fate a second time."

"There is no hope of redemption without the shedding of blood," said Father. "It is simply unavoidable."

"One may avoid it if one does not participate."

"I drew my sword in Kansas when the pro-slavery forces attacked us, and I will never sheathe it until this war is over," said Father, his voice rising.

"You may die, then, with your sword unsheathed," said Salmon.

"I would rather see a whole generation of men, women, and children sacrificed than have liberty perish from the earth."

Father's voice rang out as if he were delivering a sermon in church, and it was overpowering in our small home.

Salmon stopped in front of Father, chin out, eyes flashing.

"The trip to Harpers Ferry is not wise. It is a mistake, and I will not take part in it," he said.

If Father was stubbornly fixed in his opinion, he had raised his children to be likewise, and he had met his match in Salmon. He stood up to face his son. He looked small and pallid, but the ferocity of his will made him seem to tower over Salmon. Father's silence was so threatening that I thought he might strike, but Salmon did not back down.

Finally, with an unnerving calm, Father said, "I have never before criticized the act of any of my children, but I am deeply and bitterly disappointed by your decision."

None of us had ever defied Father. He had struck my brothers to discipline them, but never could I remember any of us openly refusing to do what he said. Fathers were supposed to be right. They were supposed to know what was best for their children and to protect them against harm. Good fathers did these things. Was John Brown a good father? I thought of the Bible story of Abraham and his only son Isaac, how Abraham believed God was telling him to take Isaac to a mountaintop and kill him to prove his love and devotion to God. When Isaac realized what his father had to do, he trusted Abraham and accepted his fate. After all, the command was coming from God. Lucky for Isaac, God stopped Abraham before he plunged the knife into his son's heart. I wondered what would have happened if, like Salmon, Isaac had refused to go with his father. Most likely, they both would have been gravely punished. Was God asking Father to sacrifice his sons at Harpers Ferry? Father's religious convictions were so strong that if he felt he was being directed by God, I knew he'd stop at nothing to fulfill the divine command. I waited, breathless, to hear what the others would say.

Father sat back in his chair and studied the faces of the other men and then lighted on Watson.

"You have done well to stay at Timbucto and watch over the family, Watson," he said, "for which I am ever grateful. But now you're called to a greater task. Are you up for it?"

I glanced at Belle beside me. She pressed her lips together. A solid woman, Belle was a good match for Watson. Watson could handle oxen, heave hay into the loft, and fell trees, but he was slow, and the action Father had planned looked like it would call for quick thinking.

Watson was frowning, and I could tell he was weighing his decision.

"Will you give me tonight to sleep on it?" he asked.

"We must not shrink from fighting for liberty," said Father. "Our plan is right in itself, and a night of sleep will not change it."

Without looking at Belle, Watson replied, "Then yes, Father, I'll go with you."

Belle lowered her head and slowly walked back to the kitchen. My heart ached for her, but I trembled with worry over what would happen to Watson.

"When is this event supposed to happen, Mr. Brown?" asked Lyman Epps.

"I hope to act right away," he said, looking at Mr. Epps. "Can I count on you?"

"Mr. Brown," said Lyman Epps, "I'm lucky enough never to have known slavery. I feel for my kinsmen, and I hope you win the war against the slave owners. But as for me—I own my land, I work when I want, I rest when I want. I'm free, and my children are free. I can do far more by being the living fulfillment of the dream of every black man and woman in America than I can lying dead on a battlefield in Harpers Ferry. North Elba is where I belong, and North Elba is where I'm going to stay."

"I see your point," said Father. I was surprised he didn't give Mr. Epps an argument.

He turned to Henry Thompson. He had been Father's captain during the war in Kansas, and Ruth nearly lost her mind with worry.

"You've been my most loyal soldier," Father said. "Surely you're up for another run at the oppressors."

Ruth spoke up. "I can't bear the thought of Henry leaving again," she said. "It was hard enough to get along without him once."

"Ruth, you may come," said Father. "I'll arrange for a farmhouse outside Harpers Ferry, and we'll need women to help with the household duties."

"No," said Ruth. Her face was flushed, but her reply was immediate and firm.

"We must all endure hardships for the sake of the poor and despised to put an end to their suffering," said Father.

"When I think of all the African women deprived of both husband and children, I feel deeply for them," said Ruth. "I would go almost anywhere with Henry if I could do them good, but . . ." Her voice broke off and she covered her face with her hands.

Henry rubbed his finger beside his aristocratic nose. He was strong and intelligent, and I could see why Father would want him in his army.

"I was with you, sir," he said, "when I thought your mission was to lead the slaves to freedom. What you have devised will end in war."

I had heard talk of war between the states, but it had always been something distant and not of my concern. Surely Henry was exaggerating. It was hard for me to believe that the actions of one man—even if he was John Brown—could cause civil war.

Father stared at Henry. Outside the window a mourning dove called.

"In a life of nearly sixty years, this is my greatest opportunity to see justice done," said Father. "I might not yet have another."

"Some say you've lost your senses," said Henry.

"That I'm mad? It may be so, but the greater insanity is one man declaring another his property. If I have lost my senses, then so has the entire country."

"If you follow this action, you'll lead your men to their deaths. And, if you manage to survive, you'll hang," said Henry, daring to put my worst fears into words.

"So be it," Father said. "Perhaps my death will send a stronger message against bondage than I could deliver in life."

"But my death will have little impact on anyone," Henry said. He looked at Ruth. "Except my family." Ruth went to her husband and faced Father with him.

"I'm with you in spirit, sir," said Henry. "And I hope to God you can effect the freedom and survival of every black man, woman, and child in America, but my allegiance is to my wife and my home. I must give up going."

Father sighed. "I did not think it like you to abandon the fight," he said.

The word "fight" hung in the air, heavy and dense as fog. Henry said nothing else; he would not go.

"I'll join you, Mr. Brown." Dauphin broke the silence so abruptly that I jumped. "I may not be your most able officer, but I will serve you well."

Oh, no, Dauphin, my mind screamed. You have no idea what you're getting yourself into. And what will I do in North Elba without you? The surge of despair I felt made me understand what Ruth, Belle, and Abbie were going through. Suddenly Harpers Ferry became my problem, my concern too, in a way that none of Father's previous plans ever had. The worry I had felt for my brothers deepened into a dread that made me feel weak. I had never questioned the way Father fought slavery, but now I, like Salmon and Henry, saw disaster looming.

"You are welcome, Dauphin," said Father. "I'm proud to have you among us."

It was done. Dauphin was recruited—he was a soldier against slavery. I remembered the vision of Father lying wounded and bandaged. Dauphin was not there by his side, nor were my brothers. What was to happen to them? I didn't know if I could change what I had seen, but I did know that I could do nothing if I stayed in North Elba.

Oliver was the only one left. He was a scholar, not a fighter. He was the youngest of John Brown's sons, and he had a new wife. Surely he would not go, not with so much to lose.

"I would serve you again, Father," he said slowly, "but I am drawn to stay in North Elba."

I felt relieved until Father's eyes took on a knowing look.

"Martha can come too," he said. "I can assure you that she will be safe."

Slowly Oliver looked at Martha, who had come into the parlor. She was sixteen, barely a woman, and in her face I could see her love for my brother. Her large brown eyes brimmed with tears, but she smiled when she looked at Oliver. Then she nodded her head.

"We'll go, Father," Oliver said softly.

Dauphin, Oliver, and now Martha—the three people dearest to me in the world—had committed to go. I made my decision—I would go too. Perhaps, I thought, my fears will fade and I will help strike a blow against slavery. If not, I had no idea of what I could do, but I would not stand by and watch Dauphin, Watson, and Oliver be sacrificed, not even for the cause of abolition.

"Father," I spoke up. "What about me?"

"Anna?" he said. "What can you offer?"

"Martha will need help with the cooking and washing."

"We don't need distractions," he said.

"I could be of great assistance."

He looked at me a long time. Then he said, "I suppose a woman doing her needlework on the porch would give the appearance of a calm home life. Are you volunteering?"

My heart felt ready to burst. "Yes," I said.

"You'll be called upon to labor harder than you may find agreeable."

"I can."

"It could be dangerous."

"I'm aware."

He stood and touched my cheek.

"I'm sure we'll find you of some value," he said.

I looked at Father, and his passion and commitment seemed to flow into me. For a moment I believed that with him in charge, all would be well. The price was too great for it to be otherwise. Then I looked away, and my dread returned.

When I went back into the kitchen, I found Mother sitting on a wooden chair, her head bowed, hands folded in her lap.

"Mother?" I said.

She didn't move, and her silence told me she must have heard every word.

Oliver and Father would go ahead of us and make the arrangements for renting a house. That would give Watson, Martha, and me time to pack and to see that Mother and the others had everything they'd need while we were gone. Dauphin would come later.

Before he left with Oliver, Father inspected the farm animals, the fields, the fences, as he had done each time he came home. But more than once I found him standing by the big rock in front of the house, running his hand over the rough surface of the gray stone.

When the men had packed up their belongings, Martha and I rode with them to the stagecoach station.

"From now on," Father said, "you'll answer to Isaac Smith."

"Who's Isaac Smith?" I asked.

"He's a businessman," he said, "procuring cattle in Virginia and Maryland for his ranch in New York. You'll recognize him when you see him." Father smiled. "He looks very much like your father." He climbed into the coach and Oliver followed, closing the door behind him.

"I'll come for you," Oliver called out the window.

"And we'll be ready," Martha replied.

The driver shook the reins and the horses lurched forward. Martha and I watched until the stagecoach disappeared over a hill.

Chapter 6

"A woodchuck's been at the collards again," said Salmon. "We get precious little greens as it is—there's not enough to share with the fur-bearing population."

"Maybe I can scare him away," I said. I was impatient with waiting and looked for any distraction I could find to help pass the time until Oliver came.

The slingshot, which I had whittled with a hunting knife and strung with a piece of rubber, would be just the tool to take care of the woodchuck. I tromped out to the edge of the field and gathered a small pile of stones, round as I could find them, the perfect shape for a straight shot. Then I took a seat on a stump. If I waited long enough, the varmint would be back. Meantime, I let the sun soak into me.

Presently a brown lump waddled across a furrow, heading straight for the greens. I wasted no time fixing a rock on the sling, took aim, and let it fly.

Thwap! I scored a clean hit on the woodchuck's hind end, not hard enough to do much harm through its thick fur, but enough to get his attention. He lumbered off toward the woods, looking, I hoped, for an easier field to pillage.

"You're pretty good with a slingshot." Dauphin came up behind me. When I turned around, I saw that he had a rifle under his arm, oiled barrel pointing toward the ground. "But if you're going to Harpers Ferry, you'd best know how to handle a gun."

"What makes you think I don't know how to handle a gun?" I said, eyeing the rifle. It had a powder cap, not like the old flintlock my grandfather used and which now stood in a corner of the barn, rusting.

"I didn't think you'd had the opportunity," Dauphin said. I hadn't, but not for lack of ambition. Father said hunting led to loafing, so we raised our meat or bought and traded with our neighbors. With so many brothers, any necessary shooting, like scaring bears and bobcats away from a new calf, or keeping foxes out of the henhouse, was left to them. My responsibilities involved weeding and chopping. Mother tried hard to teach me the womanly chores, but shooting had been omitted from my education, an oversight I was ready and willing to correct.

"Maybe that woodchuck will come back," said Dauphin.

"Shooting one of them's about as sporting as hitting old Ruby in the corral," I said. "Besides, you can't eat them."

"Last fall I shot one that Mother stewed with some potatoes and turnips. You cook him long enough, he tenders up."

A woodchuck did not whet my appetite, but I was aching to hold the gun.

"How does it work?" I asked, reaching for it. Dauphin took a step back.

"It's just for small animals—rabbits and squirrels. Don't go trying to kill a deer with it."

When he held it toward me, I felt such a rush of excitement that I could hardly breathe. I fumbled with it, trying to figure out which shoulder to press the butt against.

"Like this," he said, pointing me sideways and fixing the rifle against my right shoulder, adjusting my left hand under the barrel. I peered down the site at the trunk of a broad pine, my finger curled around the cold steel trigger. One squeeze, just a little pressure with one finger, would set off an explosion that could kill. I thought about the rifles in the armory at Harpers Ferry. What were they like? Did the slaves know any more about how to use one than I did? Maybe that would be Dauphin's job—to teach them how to shoot. But they wouldn't be aiming at woodchucks. I didn't want to think about it—not now anyway.

Dauphin's arms were folded across his chest. "Think you can hit anything?" he asked.

"Only one way to know," I said and started toward the woods with the rifle.

Pine needles carpeted the forest path, and through the leaves the sun spotted the rocks and ferns with splotches of light. Crows cawed in the distance, and I could hear Dauphin's soft footfall behind me. As usual, he said little. Like Oliver, Dauphin seemed comfortable with silence, and so we walked along and listened for skittering noises.

"Stop," Dauphin whispered. I jerked to a halt and swiveled my head at him. He was looking into the woods to the right of the path. "Over there."

It was a rabbit, big and gray. It had seen us and stood frozen against a tree stump. I lifted the rifle to my shoulder, my eye following the line down the barrel to the floppy-eared animal.

"Pull back the hammer," Dauphin said. "Be gentle."

The two knobs on the tip of the barrel framed the rabbit's chest where its fur vibrated with its rapid heartbeat. Dauphin put a hand under the heavy barrel to help steady it. His other hand was on my shoulder, and I could feel him close behind me.

"Make it quick," he murmured. "He'll never feel it."

The rabbit sat motionless, eyes staring back at me, innocent, defenseless, looking at death through the opening of a long-barrel rifle. My finger froze on the trigger just long enough for the rabbit to make its move, and in a flash it sprang into the brush.

"Annie," said Dauphin, letting go of the gun, of me. "If you can't shoot a rabbit, how do you expect to hold up when you're facing the enemy?" I could hear exasperation in his voice, and I didn't like him thinking poorly of me.

"I . . . I just wasn't ready," I stammered. "I'll get the next one." Dauphin reached for the rifle, but I held onto it.

"You're not ready for Harpers Ferry," he said. "You just proved that."

"Martha's going," I argued, "with Father's blessing. And she's just a year older than me."

"The house is going to be filled with arms and ammunition and an infantry of men."

I suddenly realized Dauphin was just as worried about me as I was about him. He didn't want anything to happen to me at Harpers Ferry, and the only way he could protect me was to try and convince me not to go. That's why he brought the rifle over. How could I tell him that the greater torture would be sitting at Timbucto and wondering what was happening to him and my brothers? I'd have to show him I was capable of taking care of myself.

"And there will be two women," I said. "We've been recruited the same as you. Now let's go find us something to shoot."

We walked along the path the way we had come. When we emerged into the open field, a flock of black-necked geese was busy pecking between the furrows of the wheat field. I glanced around for Dauphin, who was several paces behind me, and, without waiting for him to catch up, I took aim at a fat goose that had wandered a distance from his fellows. This time when my finger curled around the trigger, I didn't hesitate.

Dauphin stayed for dinner that night.

"I believe this is the best goose I've ever had," he said.

"Annie cleaned and plucked it herself," said Mother.

"And what have you done with all the feathers?" asked Salmon.

"I've saved them," I said. "I'm sure I'll find some use for them."

"I need a pillow," Dauphin offered. He said in his family the children took their pillows with them when they got married, and his father still slept with the one from his childhood. Dauphin was the eighteenth child, and his mother hadn't gotten around to making him one.

"If you're willing, I would pay you for it," he said. The Thompson farm was doing well. They had enough land to burn an area for charcoal, which they sold in town, and Dauphin could probably afford to buy a pillow. The money would come in handy, but I had no idea how to go about making one. Of course, I wasn't about to admit that to Dauphin.

"I hope it will meet with your approval, Mr. Thompson," I said.

Martha gave me a lesson in pillow-making, and I sat in the parlor with the bag of feathers on one side of me and a muslin case on my lap. My fingers were sweating, and when I peeled the feathers from the quill, I had to shake them off my sticky skin into the muslin. So many feathers, but a whole goose only filled half the case. I had to finish it off with chicken feathers, all colors—red, orange, some even green. Dauphin wouldn't know the difference. Feathers were feathers, and they wouldn't honk or cluck when he rested his head on them.

I stripped soft feather after soft feather, dropped the sharp quill into a sack, the down into the muslin case. When the bag was almost full, I pictured Dauphin putting his head on the pillow and wondered if he would dream of me.

I'd about worn my eyes out watching down the road for Oliver, and when he finally came, I was ready. My things had been packed for a week—my best dress for Sunday meeting, a clean homespun petticoat, an apron, an extra pair of cotton stockings, and my most beloved possession, a book Oliver gave me for my birthday— *Romeo and Juliet* by William Shakespeare.

Oliver stayed the night, long enough for us to pack the parcels Mother had prepared: a sack of grain, an iron kettle, two quilts, and a basket of bedding, among which I saw Mother lay lace doilies her mother had made and which she treasured. She hadn't said much about our going. When Father was around, she tended to her household duties and kept so closely to herself that I sometimes thought she feared him more than any of her children did. But I knew she loved each of us, and if we were to live in a strange house for a while, then she must have wanted it to feel like a real home.

It wasn't until early the next morning that I remembered I hadn't said good-bye to Dauphin, but Watson would bring him within a week, along with Dauphin's brother Will.

Martha sat up next to Oliver on the wagon, and I nestled in the back among the bundles. Day was just dawning, and the tall pines were silhouetted against the pale sky. Oliver shook the reins and the horse struggled to get the heavy wagon moving.

A confusion of emotions swirled inside me. I was leaving half my family and traveling to a place I'd never been. I questioned the soundness of my father's plan, and yet I was going to help him carry it out. I had my whole life ahead of me, but I was aware of the dangers that might cut it short. As much as what I was doing felt wrong, I knew it was right. And, above all, I knew that, whatever the outcome, nothing would ever be the same.

I turned to the prologue of *Romeo and Juliet* to find some comfort. It was a love story after all, wasn't it?

> Two households both alike in dignity
> (In fair Verona where we lay our scene)
> From ancient grudge break to new mutiny,
> Where civil blood makes civil hands unclean.

Mutiny. Civil blood. Shakespeare's words did anything but quiet my anxieties.

Chapter 7

The wagon jolted along the narrow route through the Adirondacks. Whiteface Mountain moved slowly by us until it vanished behind rock cliffs looming on either side of the road. I had lived in North Elba for the past four years, but now that I was leaving, I saw as if for the first time the furry evergreen trees, the round, friendly maples, the solid oaks. Wild daisies and Indian paintbrush adorned the woods, and the fresh aroma of spruce and summer blossoms perfumed the air.

The rutted road led steadily out of the mountains, through Elizabethtown and down toward Lake Champlain. At Westport we boarded a teamboat ferry. Two Morgan horses walked in a circle on the deck, their harnesses strapped to bars that turned the gears below deck and drove the paddlewheel.

As the boat pulled away from shore, I looked back at New York. Whiteface Mountain stared down at us, its rock outcropping shining silver in the sun. It would be there when I returned, but for now I tore my eyes away and watched the water froth over the paddlewheel behind the boat.

In Vermont we followed the road south along the railroad tracks, flaming tiger-lilies bordering our route. Brown cows munched lazily in fields, and behind tumble-down stone walls, gnarled apple trees reached out their bony limbs. The farther we got from North Elba, the less I thought of the mountains, the valleys, the log house at Timbucto.

The first night we stopped in Middlebury, unhooked the horse and slept under the wagon in case of rain. By the second night we were south of Bennington, just over the Massachusetts line. We had eaten the food Belle packed—fried chicken, hardtack biscuits, pickled beets, and hard-boiled eggs. I didn't sleep well, my stomach keeping me awake with its growling. No one else complained, though, and so I imagined a plate filled with potatoes and rolled off to sleep.

When Martha poked me, the sun was not yet up.

"Rain's setting in," she said. "We have to make some time."

I moaned. "We won't get wet under the wagon. We can wait for it to stop."

"Father will be anxious about us," said Oliver. "We have to keep moving."

I climbed into the wagon, settled against the grain sack, and pulled a blanket around me. The last thing I remembered was Oliver's voice saying, "Maybe we can make it to Springfield before we get a drenching."

A crack of thunder brought me out of a sound sleep. Raindrops pelted my face, and I pulled the blanket tighter around me. Martha had her shawl over her head, and my stalwart brother sat straight-backed in the driving rain.

Brick buildings on both sides of us, some of them four stories high, made a wide alley through which Oliver directed the horse. We must have reached Springfield. He stopped at a corner in front of a tavern with a sign that said "P. J. Bartholomew's Inn." I hopped over the side and dashed under the awning by the front door while Oliver helped Martha down from the wagon.

Inside, two men sat at a long wooden bar drinking from mugs. A yellow glow of oil lamps filtered through sweet smoke from pipe tobacco. A man approached us. He was tall and handsome and had skin the color of oiled leather. He wore a clean shirt with sleeves rolled up to his elbows and a white linen towel tied around his waist like an apron.

"Wet out there?" he asked.

"Yes," said Oliver. "We're soaked through."

"I'm Caesar," he said. "How about some hot tea and something to eat?"

"Good idea," said Oliver, much to my pleasure.

I held the blanket around me and shivered. It was summer, but rainy mornings were cool enough to chill to the bone. Caesar brought a pot of tea, and when he placed it on the table, I noticed scars on his wrists. I wondered if he had been a fugitive.

"You traveling far?" asked Caesar.

"Virginia," said Oliver.

Caesar frowned. "That's slave country." He looked worried.

"We're in the business of stopping slavery," Oliver assured him. "Have you heard of John Brown?"

"I should say so," said Caesar. "Frederick Douglass

spoke in Springfield last month, and he made mention of Mr. Brown's work in Kansas. Do you know him?"

"My name is Oliver," he said, extending his hand. "Oliver Brown. And this is my wife Martha, and my sister Annie."

"Well, now," said Caesar. "Pleased to meet you."

"Do the slave catchers give you any trouble?" asked Oliver.

"Not so long as Mr. Bartholomew is on the premises. I've been a free man for ten years, worked here for six, but that don't make a difference to some people."

"Good luck to you, Caesar," said Oliver.

I hadn't realized how hungry I was, but when Caesar brought eggs, sausage pungent with sage, and crisp bread to slather with butter and raspberry jam, I ate as if it had been days since my last meal. Then I washed it all down with another cup of tea, thick with sweet milk.

"We can't afford to do this every day," said Oliver. "But under the circumstances, a hot meal seemed prudent." Martha smiled gratefully at him.

I glanced toward the window. "Looks like the rain has let up," I said.

Oliver motioned to Caesar.

"If we can settle our bill here, we'll be back on the road," he said.

"Nothing to settle, Mr. Brown," said Caesar. "Any kin to John Brown is a guest in this establishment." Then he put a loaf of bread on the table.

"This should get you through to your next meal," he said.

The bread had been delicious, and I picked up the loaf, looking forward to nibbling on it throughout the day.

"Thank you kindly," Oliver replied.

When we got up to go, through the window I saw another wagon pull up. A plump man with a bushy mustache checked a bundle in the back and then started toward the tavern. As we walked out, he barged through the door, knocking into Martha.

"So sorry," she said. He mumbled something and kept walking.

We had to pass his wagon to get to ours, and as we did, I saw the bundle in the back move. Then it groaned.

"Oliver," I said, "I think someone's under this canvas."

When Oliver drew back the cloth, a black and red pulp pulled away from the light, clinking chains as it moved. I wasn't sure it was human. One eye was swollen shut, and dried blood caked his head. His lips were dry and cracked, and manacles had rubbed his wrists until skin hung from them in hunks. A chain led from his hands to iron bands around his ankles, and his feet were raw and covered with mud. Scratches criss-crossed his bare chest, and what was left of his pants was in tatters. My breakfast suddenly felt sour in my stomach.

Martha got the canteen from our wagon and held it to the man's lips. He hesitated, searching her face with his one good eye, and then slowly he allowed her to pour water into his mouth. She wiped his face with the sleeve of her dress and gave him more to drink.

"You a runaway?" Oliver asked.

The man gave Oliver a look that could not deny the truth.

"Damned slave catchers," Oliver said.

It had stopped raining, but my face was wet. It couldn't have been tears; I didn't remember the last time I'd cried.

Martha broke off a piece of the bread I was holding and fed it to the man.

"Thank you," he said.

"Where's he taking you?" asked Oliver.

The black man shook his head. "Auction block, I suspect."

"That devil," said Oliver. "Keep this water under the cover." He pushed the canteen under the tarp.

"And the bread," I added. I'd lost my taste for it. Oliver hid the loaf by the water.

"God bless," said the man.

"Can't we take him with us?" asked Martha.

Oliver looked toward the tavern. "That scoundrel would catch up to us in no time," he said. "And he'd be likely to shoot us all."

Just then the tavern door opened and the slave catcher came out, scowling and wiping his mustache with the back of a hand.

"I'll thank you to get away from my wagon," he said.

Oliver glared at him. "How can you in good conscience treat another human this way?"

"Human?" he scoffed. "All I see is a piece of property. Valuable property, at that."

"Is it necessary to beat him, man?" said Oliver.

"This here's a slave," said the man. "My slave now. The law says I can beat him in order to teach him how a slave behaves. That's what I done. He won't be running away no more." He pulled the cover back over the man in the wagon. "You best keep to your own business if you know what's good for you." He went back into the tavern, shutting the door with a crash behind him.

As we rode out of Springfield, the sky lightened and raindrops glittered on the leaves. My clothes dried out and I warmed up, but I'd never before seen such a gray, cheerless day.

Chapter 8

The town of Harpers Ferry sat on a narrow neck of land where the Shenandoah and Potomac rivers flowed lazily together. A wooden railroad bridge crossed the Potomac from Maryland and ran westward past the town. In the distance the mossy Blue Ridge Mountains looked sapphire in the late morning haze.

Oliver drove through the main section of town. Saloons, hotels, shops, and houses crowded together along the two rivers and up the slope of a hill. Along Potomac Street we drove past a square brick firehouse with tall arched windows through which I could see red engines standing ready for an emergency. I felt a shudder and closed my eyes.

Swirling smoke and blazes of red rose to the sky. Alarm bells screeched, and pain shot through my stomach. I tried to focus, to see through the chaos, but I could not.

When I opened my eyes again, it was like waking from

a nightmare. The firehouse was behind us, and it was a calm July day. I'd had another vision, but I didn't know what awful conflict I had seen. Was I the only one who felt it?

"Martha . . . ," I started. She turned around, her face as pretty and unconcerned as always.

"What is it, Annie?"

"Nothing," I lied. Then a thought struck me—perhaps this upheaval was what Father's plan would bring. The idea frightened me, but I thought it best to keep my misgivings to myself, at least for now.

Farther up the street, signs marked Father's goal—the U.S. armory and munitions building. I tried to conjure up a feeling of victory, but all I sensed was dread.

Shoppers stopped and stared at us, whispering behind cupped hands. Except for the clattering of the horse's hooves on the cobblestones and the rattle of the wagon, the morning had an eerie quiet. Oliver said we were renting a place called Kennedy Farm a short ride from Harpers Ferry, just across the river in Maryland. I hoped we'd get there soon.

Larch trees with shabby trunks crowded the road to the farm. Warm, damp air and the thick aroma of honeysuckle made me feel drowsy. We stopped at a rickety split-rail fence, and Oliver jumped down from the wagon to swing open the gate. Above the overgrown bushes I glimpsed a tall log house with a drooping porch running half way across the second level, and the white filling between the logs was worn away in places. It must have been a while since anyone had lived there.

Oliver led the horse and wagon up the drive, past a grassless yard where chickens pecked amid rusting farm tools. Across the drive a roughly built shed, half concealed by thick shrubbery, settled into muddy ground.

Owen, robust and cheerful, came to greet us. His bushy beard compensated for what had receded from his forehead, and it made him look larger and stronger than I remembered.

"We've been expecting you," he said loudly. "Good trip?"

He looked around as he spoke. Then he said soft enough so his voice wouldn't carry beyond us, "We're the Smiths, helping our father conduct cattle business. Townsfolk have been driving by." He nodded his head toward the road. "I wouldn't be surprised to have one or two stop in for a neighborly visit before long."

"Is Father here?" I asked.

"Inside," said Owen.

He led us toward the house. We entered through a door under the porch and followed him up a narrow flight of stairs to the main room. Light filtered through grimy windows and floated in through an open door leading to the porch.

Father leaned over his desk, pointing at papers and talking in a low voice with a man who was dressed for the city. The man looked up, but the papers held Father's attention.

"I'm Jeremiah Anderson." He nodded first to Martha and then to me. He was clean-shaven and smelled of hair oil. Father had recruited people of class, it appeared.

At last Father walked around the desk, still holding the papers in his hand.

"Oliver's wife Martha and my daughter Annie," he said simply.

"When we were in Kansas," said Mr. Anderson,

"Osawatomie Brown talked about your strength of character."

Was he speaking to me? Why had Father never told me that he thought I was strong?

"Strong-willed, I believe I said," Father corrected.

"You wouldn't mean hard-headed, would you?" Owen said.

I felt relieved that they were able to laugh, even if it was at my expense. I had expected the same serious tone as at the meeting at Timbucto.

"You may find our mining operation a little cramped once the other miners arrive with all their tools," Mr. Anderson said.

Miners and tools? He must have been warning me to learn the code and use it at all times. We had to make sure no one suspected why we were really there.

"I'll show you the house and where you'll sleep." Oliver gestured toward the staircase.

Martha and I followed Oliver downstairs. The house was nearly twice the size of Timbucto. The kitchen occupied the ground level with a pantry in the back. My room was off the main area, as was Father's, and Martha would sleep in a back room with Oliver. Owen and Mr. Anderson would stay in the loft, an open space on the top floor big enough for a battalion of men to sleep.

It was a comfortable house, although it lacked a woman's care. The windows would have to be washed, and the floors needed scrubbing, but if we recruited a man or two to help us, Martha and I could make the place homey in a short time. At least that's what I wanted to believe. But I couldn't dispel the vision I'd seen in Harpers Ferry. Something still was not right, and I had a feeling I'd find out soon enough what it was.

Chapter 9

In the next week Martha enlisted Oliver and Owen to mend broken chairs and repair cupboard hinges. I washed windows and polished furniture and then laid out Mother's doilies on the back of the sofa to cover the worn spots. Oliver strung a clothesline in the yard. Sheets and towels and ladies' things hanging on the line would be a good sign of a woman's touch around the house. We all had a hand in weeding the garden the men had planted. Already beans were ready to harvest, and summer squash, too, which never survived the cold nights of North Elba summers. I cooked most of the meals—eggs and porridge for breakfast, stews for supper—and swept the floor while Oliver and Martha washed and dried the dishes.

My new surroundings started to feel comfortable, and with all the work, I didn't have much time to worry about the future. Father didn't seem at ease, though. At Timbucto he retired early and rose before daybreak, but here I would awake in the night to hear him pacing. One morning I rose to start breakfast and found him at his desk, head resting on folded arms, sound asleep. He was always tense, like a wire coiling to spring. Our neighbor, Mrs. Huffmaster, may have helped to wind the coil tighter.

The morning I met her, I was in the front yard beating dusty rugs with a broom. I turned from the rugs hanging on the sagging clothesline and found a woman peering over the fence. Four barefoot children looked in through the lower rails.

"Haloo," yelled the woman.

My stomach jumped. This was the first test in dealing with the neighbors—I had to be very careful.

"You all just move in?" she called. She leaned on her thick arms, which were planted on the top rung of the gate.

"Yes," I said, coming closer so we didn't have to yell. "We've been here a week."

"Where abouts you come from?"

Father hadn't prepared me for questions like this. Should I tell the truth or lie?

"New York. The northern part."

"I'm Eunice Huffmaster, and these are my youngsters." The ample woman unfastened the gate and let herself and the children through. She must have taken the courtesy as an invitation to visit.

"What brings you so far south?" Mrs. Huffmaster asked.

"The weather," I said. I had rehearsed this conversation with Oliver. He said Martha and I would arouse curiosity in the neighborhood, and he was right. "The growing season is so short up north, you know."

Three of the children darted around to the back property.

"My little ones been using this place as a playhouse," she said.

"Playhouse?"

"Sure. Wasn't nobody living here. I didn't see no harm."

"Mrs. Hoff . . ."

"Huffmaster," she corrected.

"Yes," I continued. "My father is a very busy man. That is—he has important work to do. He can't be disturbed. The children . . ."

"Oh, don't you worry none about them," she said. "Say—is that white-bearded man your pappy?"

"Yes. And the other two men are my brothers." The woman eyed the porch.

"I heard your pappy was a cattleman. Word around is that he's looking to drive some fat head all the way to New York. That true?"

"Well, yes. He's making those arrangements. But it may take a while." I looked around for the missing children.

"What's your name?" said the fourth child. Sandy colored hair stuck out from under a cap, and dirt was smeared across a cheek.

Truth or lie? My mind went blank. "Uh . . . Annie. Annie . . . Smith."

"Our farm is just the other side of the church," said Mrs. Huffmaster, pointing back down the drive. "Looks like we'll be seeing a lot of each other, Annie."

"How nice." I forced a smile.

The three children came dashing back to their mother.

"There's a witch living in the house," one said.

"I'm not coming back here," said the second. The smallest, thumb stuck in his mouth, grabbed his mother's hand.

"A witch?" I said.

The first two children gave vigorous nods, and the

thumb-sucker buried his face in Mrs. Huffmaster's skirt. What strange children, I thought.

"If you'll excuse me," I said, "I'd better attend to my chores." I headed toward the house, but before I went in, I made sure Mrs. Huffmaster had closed the gate behind her with all four children in tow.

Martha was sitting on a kitchen chair staring out the rear window.

"Good thing those children showed up," she said.

"Why in the world would that make you glad?" I asked.

"I was having a dizzy spell. Acting like a madwoman took my mind off it."

So Martha was the witch.

"Got rid of them, too," I laughed. Then I realized what Martha had said.

"Dizzy spell?" I asked. If Martha was coming down sick, I'd have all the work to do myself, a prospect which I did not relish.

"Can you keep a secret?" she said, leaning toward me.

"Seems like everything's a secret in this family," I said.

"I'm going to have a baby."

"A baby?"

Martha pressed a hand against her stomach.

"Are you surprised?" she asked.

I was surprised, all right. Shocked and frightened, too. I already had a pile of uncertainties to deal with, and throwing an expectant mother on top made me more nervous. What if it didn't go well? What if Martha took ill?

"Does Oliver know?" I asked.

"No." Martha bit her lip. "I don't want to take the chance that he'll send me back. I'm sure we Brown women can keep this to ourselves."

"How long have you known?" I asked.

"A little while now, but don't worry. The baby won't come before the new year," she said. "That should get us through the raid."

Martha looked back out the window. Maybe Dauphin was right about not sending women into war—what would Father say when he found out one of his soldiers was soon to become a mother?

Chapter 10

"She's just a curious neighbor, Father. I'm sure she means no harm." I hoped I was right about Mrs. Huffmaster.

Father stood at the door and scanned the front drive, combing his beard with the fingers of one hand. I watched him walk to his desk, slowly sit down, and open a drawer. He pulled out a gray pistol, checked the chambers, and then took out a cloth. He rubbed the barrel, gently drawing the cloth over the metal, then turned the gun around and handed it to me.

"I want you to keep this close to you at all times," he said. "When you watch on the porch, keep it under your sewing. If anyone threatens you or anyone in this house, aim for the heart and pull the trigger."

My stomach turned over when I realized Father was telling me to kill someone. How would I know if killing was necessary? I wondered if Father had found it necessary to kill the proslavery men at Osawatomie and to shoot slaveowners in Missouri. Then I thought of the black man outside the tavern on our way to Maryland, saw again his swollen face, saw the cold, hard manacles on his wrists and ankles, and I knew the slave trade had to be stopped. I'd always believed that murder could not be justified by any cause, but now I wasn't so sure.

I reached for the pistol. It was a manageable size, just right for my hands. It had six chambers, each backed by a firing cap that, with a squeeze of the trigger, would discharge the ball packed inside. On the cylinder was etched a boat—two masts, square sails filled with wind, water parting under the bow. I ran my finger over the tiny cuts. Whoever had tooled the scene might laugh to know that this decorated weapon had become the possession of a fifteen-year-old girl. Tucked into the waistband of my skirt, the pistol was hidden under my apron. I had to admit I felt safer with it there.

That afternoon I sat on the front porch, as Father instructed. A warm wind was blowing and birds were chirping, but other than that it was a quiet summer afternoon. I kept an eye on the road, glancing now and then at the cross stitch on my lap. I had crossed the blue over the yellow to make the flowers green. It wasn't what I had intended. They were to be purple, but the red thread was inside in Martha's sewing basket. I would have gone in to get it, except I wouldn't leave the porch. Couldn't leave the porch. Someone might come, and I'd have to warn Father. Martha and I would take turns working on the design as we sat our watch. My hands were rough and fumbling, and each stitch was painstakingly slow, but already I could see the picture taking form—a pond with lilypads floating on it. If I looked hard enough, I could almost see into the dark water, almost detect a glint of metal from the pistol underneath. I was so focused on the loaded gun and the leafy road ahead that I had to tear out nearly as many stitches as I put into the sewing because of my mistakes. Weeding the garden would have been easier, but Martha was working in the kitchen and until she came to relieve me, I would force myself to sit and watch.

I was about to pull out another stitch when I heard hooves pounding the packed dirt on the road. A horseman galloped up to the gate at full speed as if to jump it, but the horse stopped at the last minute and reared up on its hind legs.

Before I could think, I was off the porch, down the stairs, gripping the pistol behind the apron and scattering squawking chickens as I dashed across the yard. The man took off his hat and waved it in the air.

"What's your business, sir?" I asked loudly.

He leaned forward on his saddle and looked me up and down. He was well dressed and clean-shaven, except for a trim mustache and long sideburns. His eyes glittered, and when he smiled, a gold tooth flashed.

"I'm not here to talk business with a lady," he said. "How about you just open the gate for me."

"Not until I know your purpose," I said. My hands were trembling, but I stood my ground.

"I said open the gate, little girl, or I'll get down and open it myself." The smile was gone, and his eyebrows pulled together in irritation.

"You just stay up on your mount," I said. I pulled the pistol out and held it steady with both hands. The barrel pointed in the direction of his head.

He looked startled, and then he grinned. "Your pappy

knows better than to give you a loaded gun."

It took both thumbs to pull the hammer back. Click. The breeze died and the birds were silent. His horse took a step backward.

"How about you just hand your toy over to me."

As he swung a leg over the saddle to dismount, I squeezed the trigger. Behind the horse a tree limb splintered and crashed to the ground. I'd aimed high, but now I brought the gun down so that it pointed right in the middle of his forehead.

"Whoa," he said and steadied the prancing animal. Smoke rose from the barrel of the pistol.

"You win." He held a palm toward me in surrender. "I'm John Cook."

"And?" I said.

"I'll tell you why I'm here if you'll put that gun down."

"That will teach you not to aggravate my daughter, Cook," Father said from behind me.

Mr. Cook slid down from his horse, looking relieved.

"I should have known this was the daughter of Osawatomie Brown," he said. "She's got a sure eye and a quick trigger finger."

"Should I let him in, Father?" I asked.

"I don't think he'll be any more trouble," said Father.

I opened the gate for Mr. Cook to lead his horse through, but I kept an eye out for Mrs. Huffmaster in case the shot brought her running.

"What news do you have from Harpers Ferry?" Father said to Mr. Cook.

"Good news," he said. "You can congratulate me on my newborn son." He stuck a thumb into his vest pocket proudly. "I'd break open a bottle of ale, but I know you don't touch the stuff."

"I don't see cause to congratulate you for corrupting a young girl with your insincere charm," Father said.

"I did right by her," said Cook. "She's a married woman now."

"I'm glad you've attempted to redeem yourself," said Father, frowning. I knew his scolding tone. Mr. Cook was young enough to be one of his own children.

"The boy will be the first of many, if I have my way," said Mr. Cook.

Father changed the subject. "Are you still holding the job on the canal in town?"

"I am," he said. "Not much happening on the waterfront. Harpers Ferry's a little too quiet for my taste. Almost half the town are free Negroes, and half the whites are government workers from up north. It seems to me there's more scowling between northerners and southerners than between blacks and whites."

"Have you seen any of the men come through?"

He must have meant the men who were part of the plan. I knew we were expecting a houseful.

"Not yet, but they should be showing up any day. I'm watching the stage coach and railroad stations."

"Any suspicions as far as you can tell?"

"None."

"Good." Father held the gate open. "You'd best get back to Mrs. Cook and the baby. Keep your eyes open—and your mouth shut."

Mr. Cook climbed onto his horse.

"Watch my back for me, will you, old man?" he said. "I think your daughter has it in for me."

If what Mr. Cook said was true, it looked like before long Mrs. Huffmaster wouldn't be the only company around the Kennedy farm.

Chapter 11

The first week of August Watson arrived with Dauphin and Will Thompson. It had only been a short time, but I had missed Dauphin—I hadn't realized how much until I saw him. I rushed across the living room to greet him but stopped short. I'm sure my face blushed as red as his as we stood awkwardly in front of each other. It wouldn't have been proper to throw my arms around Dauphin—not in front of the other men. A month or two before, I might not have cared what was proper or not, but things were different now. Dauphin had come to do a job, as I was doing mine. One day we might hold onto each other, but for now I was glad to see his shy grin and twinkling blue eyes.

"I hope you'll find it comfortable here, Dauphin," I said.

"I'm sure I will," he said, "especially with this." He was carrying a burlap bag from which he pulled a feather pillow.

"The one I made?" I asked.

"The only one I own," said Dauphin. "If there's to be war, at least I'll have a soft place to lay my head." Feathers and lead balls, comfort and conflict—they didn't seem to mix, but it was so like Dauphin with his gentle ways to bring a pillow to Harpers Ferry. I hoped he wouldn't have to find out what war was like—I hoped none of us would—but there was no turning the tide now. Father had set his plan in motion, and I'd never known him to run from a struggle.

Within a day, five more men arrived: Charles Tidd, Aaron Stevens, Stewart Taylor, and two brothers, Barclay and Edwin Coppoc. The men all claimed their spaces in the loft and played checkers or wrote letters. One by one they came to the kitchen to bathe away the road dust, and Martha and I washed their clothes and hung them on the line outside. It was risky to display so many shirts and trousers in the yard, but in the August heat, they would dry quickly and I could retrieve them before suspicious neighbors rode by.

When the men were settled, Father and Oliver pored over maps of Harpers Ferry and census reports of the town's population. I sat my watch on the porch and listened to their conversation through the open door.

"The best time to attack is evening," said Oliver. "No one will expect a raid in the dark."

"With any luck," said Father, "no one will expect a raid at all. You're right about the dark, though, but just before sunrise we'll find most asleep and the guard groggy at the end of his shift."

"If we could cross the river by boat and come up the bank, we might have the best chance."

"The current is too strong, and we can't risk hitting

the rocks. Coming in on foot is our best approach."

They talked on and on about options and alternatives. Even from the porch, I could feel the tension growing.

A small bird fluttered its wings in front of the door, flew in and then out again. Seconds later, the bird darted back in. This time I put my needlework down and looked into the room. The bird chirped frantically, flitted in a wide circle around the ceiling, and then swooped out over my head. Father put down his pencil and Oliver closed his book, but neither moved.

"Is anyone coming?" asked Father.

I checked the road again.

"No," I said. All was still. Ominously still.

When the little bird flew in the third time, Father pulled his sword from under the desk and started down the stairs.

"Something's wrong," he said. "I'd better check outside."

"I'll come with you," I said. I wondered why he chose his sword rather than a gun. I was ready with my pistol, just in case. Oliver watched from the porch.

The bird flew circles over Father's head and led us to a bush in a corner of the yard. There in the branches near the ground, four tiny heads, beaks wide open, bobbed in a nest.

"Oh, Father, look," I said. "It wanted us to see its babies."

"Annie—don't—move," he said.

Then I heard the rattle.

Coiled beside me, poised and ready to strike, a snake shook its tail. With a quick arc of his arm, Father raised the saber and brought it down, slicing clean through the rattlesnake. Its two ends writhed and twisted as the blood spewed out of it.

Suddenly the bright day turned black. I saw a dark night, a swift stream running through the woods, saw my father's saber rise and glisten silver in the moonlight. A man was kneeling in front of Father. Violence and hatred made the air foul. The sword fell, spilling blood. Screams rang out. The saber cut again. Life flowed out of the man—a slaveowner. Father's eyes flashed. His teeth bared in a grimace. He stood over his fallen enemy. There was no pity in his expression or his posture, only contempt.

I tried to step back, away from the vision I knew was Osawatomie, Kansas. But I had to face the truth. What I had seen was no battle or part of a moral fight against slavery. It was murder. At last I truly understood why John Brown's name struck fear in men's hearts. I, too, was afraid.

The snake and the Maryland earth rushed back into focus, and I blinked my eyes against the glare. The little bird flew back to its nest to tend its young.

"I think this is an omen," Father said. "I believe the bird was asking for my help. It must be a sign of good fortune for our project."

"I hope so, Father," I said, also hoping he wouldn't notice the quaver in my voice. Father held the saber in his right hand as if it were part of him. Obviously, Father did not believe that "Thou shalt not kill" applied to his fight against the slaveowners. I didn't doubt his motives—slavery was wrong and it had to be abolished. But how many would he kill to see it happen?

"Haloo!" I jumped. Mrs. Huffmaster was holding a cloth to the back of her neck with one hand and letting herself in through the gate with the other.

"Can anyone help with this boil? I can't take the children all the way into town just to see the barber, but it's tried me to the limit of my tolerance." She scanned the clothesline from one end to the other while she talked.

"Mrs. Huffmaster, I believe it is?" Father said, holding his hand out to her. They were bound to meet sooner or later.

"Oh, why yes," she said, eyeing the saber.

"I have some experience with the lancing of boils. Won't you come up to the house?"

Had he lost his wits? Mrs. Huffmaster wanted to have a peek at the inside of the house, I was sure of that, and she was about to get what she came for. I hoped the men were quietly tucked in the attic.

Martha sat sewing when Mrs. Huffmaster breezed in, her head pivoting to take in every detail in spite of the boil. Oliver must have dashed upstairs to alert the men, and I could imagine them still as statues.

"It's unkindly hot, Mrs. Huffmaster," said Father. "Perhaps you'd be more comfortable outside." He ushered her through the sitting room and out onto the porch before she could light on anything that might give her a clue about the real purpose of the house.

I brought a razor, some alcohol, and a clean cloth, and Father set to work on Mrs. Huffmaster's neck. Her eyes wandered over the railing and back to the clothesline.

"You men folks certainly have got a right smart lot of shirts," she said.

"Yes," said Father. "The boys and I have let the washing back up on us. Except for what we have on our backs, that amounts to every stitch of clothing we have in the world."

Mrs. Huffmaster seemed to think a minute. "Looks like you all are fine dressers."

"We try to look our best for church on Sunday," said Father. "I believe it shows respect for the Lord, don't you?"

He sliced open the boil and caught the pus with the cloth. Mrs. Huffmaster yelped and stuck the knuckle of her forefinger between her front teeth. Father cleaned the wound and taped a bandage on it.

"There," he said. "Is that better?"

She reached up and patted her neck. "Why, yes. Much better. I don't believe a surgeon could have done as well."

"Anything else we can help you with, please let us know," Father told her. I was amazed that he could be so gracious with his conspirators hidden just up the stairs.

On her way out of the yard, Mrs. Huffmaster took another long look at the men's clothes swaying on the line and then let herself through the gate.

"Annie," said Father, "keep a close eye on the road. I'm sure our neighbor will find other excuses for a visit, but if she brings anyone with her, stall them at the gate and alert me right away."

"Yes, Father," I said.

"And keep that pistol handy."

Chapter 12

Willy Leeman was only seventeen when he fought with Father at Osawatomie. He was boyish with a broad forehead and ears too large for his head, but he had sprightly eyes, and I thought him handsome. He smoked too much, though, and took nips from the flask of liquor he carried in his pocket, for which Father scolded him. Of all the men who had come to the farm, Willy was the only one who seemed to have no fear of Father, nor even a healthy respect. There was devilment about him, and I suspected that he'd make a difficult companion in a house full of hiding men.

The attic was filling up, and making meals for so many men was almost a full-time operation. I stood at the window while I cooked, one eye always on the road. After supper I sat on the porch with my needlework hiding my pistol and watched for Mrs. Huffmaster or any other curious townsfolk. A few rode up on horseback and scanned the property or yelled greetings. Maybe they were government spies. Probably they were just curious about these strange northerners who kept to themselves and never invited the neighbors in for small talk. It was worrisome nevertheless not knowing how much they really knew.

By mid-August packages began arriving. Oliver and Owen picked up large wooden boxes at the train station and brought them to the farm on the back of a wagon. Then the door to the shabby cabin was unlocked, the boxes unpacked, the door locked again. Once it was fifteen boxes of rifles and revolvers. Another time it was nearly a thousand pikes with ten-inch blades of double-edged steel.

"These are for slaves who don't know how to use guns," Father said, inspecting a spear. One way or another, Father intended to include every able-bodied black man in the struggle.

One night after the men were settled upstairs and it was quiet, I sat with Father while he wrote letters.

"Are you writing Mother?" I asked.

"Not tonight, Anna. I'm writing Frederick Douglass another request to join us."

"I hope he decides to come," I said. I'd met Mr. Douglass on a trip with Father to Springfield, Massachusetts, when I was just a young girl, but his image was burned in my memory. He was a formidable man with wild black hair and stern eyes whose brows met between them. He had escaped from slavery and traveled around the North giving abolitionist lectures. Even the coldest hearts melted under his passionate protests against slavery.

"So far he has declined," Father said. "That's why I've decided to deliver this letter in person. I'm leaving for

Chambersburg tomorrow." Father had left the farm a few times to go to town for supplies, but I was nervous when he was gone. We were sitting on a powder keg holding a slow-burning match, and we all looked to Father to tell us what to do.

"I'll be taking Owen with me," he said. "We'll be gone a week. Watson and Oliver can see to the farm duties. Just be sure the others stay out of sight."

"Must you go?" I asked.

Father put his pen down and leaned back in his chair.

"Yes, Anna. Even if Mr. Douglass declines to come, I'll need to talk with our supporters. We're even with expenses at the moment, but the raid will be more costly than we have the means."

However meagerly we lived so that every nickel could go for weapons and ammunition, Father never seemed to have enough. Our lack of money just added to the odds that were already stacked against us. I understood the importance of Father's trip—he needed someone like Mr. Douglass on his side for the raid to succeed.

Shortly after Father and Owen rode out, Oliver hooked the horse to the wagon.

"Where are you going?" I asked.

"Into town," he said. "We're expecting another shipment."

"More tools?" I asked. I'd learned the code language for the arsenal the conspirators were collecting.

"Yes," said Oliver.

"I'll come along," I offered.

Oliver looked back at the house.

"Watson can look after Martha," I said. "She has plenty of company."

I could tell he was worried, and I wondered if he suspected she was with child. He shook the reins and started the horses down the road.

The train station was by the river just outside Harpers Ferry. Oliver pulled the wagon up to the loading dock and called to the station attendant.

"Any shipments for—er—Smith?" he said.

"Smith, is it?" said the man. "I'll have a look." He wore blue cap and pants, and his white shirt had dark circles of sweat under the arms.

He disappeared into the station. Oliver hopped onto the platform and paced back and forth in front of the door. The horse shifted his weight and swished his tail. Presently the attendant backed out the door, dragging a box. It was shaped like a small coffin and jerked over the wooden planks of the platform. Then the man went back and pulled a second box just like the first into the sunlight.

"What've you got in here—andirons?" he said, puffing. He pulled a handkerchief from his pocket and mopped his forehead.

"Bibles," said Oliver.

"Beg pardon?"

"My father's a preacher back in New York," he lied. "He's donating Bibles to the church in our community."

"I don't know," said the attendant. "Pretty heavy for Bibles. We better pry off the tops and see if you got the right shipment. Be right back with the crow bar."

He went into the station again.

"Oliver," I urged, "don't let him open the crate."

"Help me get them loaded," he said. The attendant was right—the boxes of rifles were much heavier than one would expect books to be. I pulled while Oliver pushed, and we

78

managed to get the second crate onto the wagon bed just as the attendant came back with a metal bar.

"No need to bother now," said Oliver, "especially in this heat." He handed the man a coin. "You've been very helpful."

"I didn't know the word of God carried so much weight," said the attendant.

"Have a lovely afternoon, sir," I said, giving him my sweetest smile. Oliver turned the wagon back toward the farm.

"That was close," he whispered.

Coming back, the wagon did not escape Mrs. Huffmaster's attention, and she strolled up as I opened the gate for Oliver. I occupied her by the fence while Oliver and Watson unloaded the boxes into the shed.

"Big load of cargo you got there," she said.

I had to think quickly.

"My mother has decided to join us." I mustered as much enthusiasm as I could. "She boxed up the furniture and is sending it ahead of her a piece at a time."

"Why don't you just take it on into the house?" She crossed her arms over her large breasts.

I had to come up with a good answer.

"You'd have to know my mother. If we didn't arrange the furniture exactly as she wanted it, she'd be very upset. It's better to let her do the unpacking."

"Well, now," said Mrs. Huffmaster. "Your mother sounds like a right smart woman. I imagine her and me'll get along just fine."

I wondered what Mother would think of our nosy neighbor. "Be not a companion of fools," Father always advised, but I was forced to make an exception with Mrs. Huffmaster.

Chapter 13

While Father was gone, I slept in the front room with the pistol by my pillow. If intruders came, I wanted to be ready. My nights were restless, though, and at every rustling I rose to look out at the locked shed and the lonely road.

The sound of crickets chirping drifted through the open window. The stars seemed farther away than in North Elba, and the moonlight cast a pale glow over the front yard, looking almost like an early frost at Timbucto. I wondered how Sarah and Ellen were. Sarah had probably taken over my chores and most likely was helping Salmon dig potatoes and pull carrots. I imagined Mother, worrying about her family so far away. I so hoped we'd all be home before long. We would have much to celebrate— the freedom of the slaves and the riches of the harvest. Every now and then I allowed myself to think about my visions, though, and the sick sense of a coming disaster would wash over me.

One night I dreamed an angry beast with teeth like bayonets had backed me against a cold stone wall. He crept closer, his metallic breath hot against my face, and his teeth dripped with blood. Through a small window behind him, morning was breaking in a fiery sunrise, and I screamed. I awoke in a sweat, the hard steel of the gun against my cheek, and for a moment I was not sure whether I was awake or still dreaming. When I heard the door under the front stairs creak open, I sat up and looked around. It was almost daybreak and light enough to see the chairs and Father's desk, and I knew I was no longer asleep. Hammer cocked, I gripped the pistol and waited on the top step. In the dark stairwell I could make out a form, the musk smell of swamp coming from it.

"Who is it?" I growled.

"It's Owen," came the reply.

I heaved a breath of relief and released the hammer. In the faint light I could make out Owen's bushy beard. When he came into the room, another man was behind him. This one was smaller but well-built and dark-skinned.

"This is the Emperor," Owen said.

"Emperor?" I said. I wasn't sure I understood him.

"Son of an African prince sold into slavery," said Owen.

"Also known as Shields Green," the black man added. He shook his head. "What a time we had getting here."

"Mr. Douglass was hiding the Emperor in Chambersburg," Owen said. "The slave catchers got wind he was there, so we started out ahead of Father and traveled by night."

"Right on our tail, they was," said the Emperor.

"We took to the woods and they followed us for a while.

Then I heard them say they were going back for reinforcements."

"Your brother here, he wanted me to swim with him across the river, but I told him, Emperor can't swim."

"What did you do?" I asked.

"He swam 'cross the river with me on his back," Mr. Green said. "And him with a crippled arm. I never seen the like." Owen had a withered arm, which I never paid any mind. He was as strong as other men with two good arms.

The Emperor was in his mid-twenties with skin like rich velvet. In Africa people would bow down to him, but here he was chased like a criminal.

"Sit down, Emperor," I said, "and I'll fix you a breakfast fit for royalty."

The Emperor was the first black man to join Father's army. The following night Dangerfield Newby found his way to the farm. He was over six feet tall, a graying mulatto with wide eyes and whiskers on his chin. He told us that his owner, who was also his father, had freed his brothers and sisters, but he had sold Mr. Newby's wife, Harriet, and their six children to a Virginia plantation owner.

"Soon's we've done our business here," he said in a voice smooth as syrup, "I'll be heading south to snatch my family out of slavery."

I couldn't condemn him for wanting to steal what was rightfully his. After all, it was a small crime compared to what the white man had done to Mr. Newby's people. Getting to know Mr. Newby and the Emperor, I was beginning to see why Father was so set on carrying through with his plan. He would resort to desperate measures to help these people have the freedom they deserved. But could it be gained any other way?

When Father finally drove the wagon up, he had a fair-skinned Negro with him, not the famed black man we expected. I waited until he had put down his things to ask my burning question.

"Where's Frederick Douglass, Father? Is he coming later?"

Father frowned. I wished I hadn't asked.

"Mr. Douglass sees fit to find his own means toward abolition," he said. "He could not be persuaded to come with us." He sifted through some papers on his desk.

From what I'd heard, slaves who wouldn't follow a white man into rebellion—not even Osawatomie Brown— would march into battle if Frederick Douglass were leading them. Surely Father knew that there was little chance of his plan succeeding without Douglass there to rally the slaves. The faint sense of hope that I had tried to nurture since arriving in Virginia vanished. Father, however, was not to be discouraged.

"Chatham Anderson here is ready to put on his armor, and I thank God for such an able recruit," said Father.

Osborn Perry Anderson preferred to be called Chatham. He was born in Pennsylvania, but he moved to Canada to work at a newspaper in Chatham, Ontario, he explained. He was a bachelor with intelligent eyes and a pile of books under his arm.

"Mr. Anderson's a schoolteacher in Canada, Anna," said Father. "He could help you with some lessons while we're here."

I didn't know how I'd find time for reading with all my duties around the farm, but I looked eagerly at the books. Chatham must have read my face.

"You may borrow any of my books, Miss Brown," he said, "long as you take good care of them. When I was a boy I sometimes went hungry so I could use whatever money I had to buy them." He stacked the volumes on Father's desk. "Right now," he said, "knowledge is the only power the black man has."

Chatham made sixteen at the Kennedy farm, not counting Martha and me. Early every morning before breakfast Father gathered the men for a worship service, while Martha or I sat on the porch to watch for passers-by. Dangerfield Newby's deep baritone anchored Aaron Stevens' ringing tenor, and they filled the house with such sweet tones that anyone hearing them would find it hard to believe that these men were planning such a violent action. But in the meantime, I listened to the choir of masculine voices, black and white, singing in harmony, and felt goose bumps tingle up and down my spine. Father ended with a prayer, always asking God to deliver the slaves from bondage.

In spite of Father's attempt to keep spirits up, the work load tripled for Martha and me. Her energy was draining into the growing baby, and she had to rest during the day, which meant even more work for me. It was hard enough to keep so many men hidden, and stress was rubbing my nerves raw.

On Sunday Father said some time out of the house would be good medicine for me, and he offered to take me to church, which I eagerly accepted. He instructed the men to stay in the loft just to be safe, even though most of the neighborhood would be at the church. Owen, Watson, Oliver, and Martha would keep an eye on things.

Isaac Smith ushered his daughter into the front pew. I saw a few raised eyebrows as we passed up the aisle, but not a single black face. In our church back home, Father always added a mix of color to the congregation, usually seated in our pew. The sanctuary was smaller than the one in North Elba, and even with the door and windows open, the heat made trickles of sweat run down the sides of my face.

A hefty man with wide sideburns led the singing, but when time came to preach the sermon, he said, "As you know, Reverend Summerhill is ministering to his ailing mother. If anyone feels moved to deliver a message this morning, come right on up to the pulpit."

Father stirred beside me. I was horrified. He wasn't going to speak, was he? I'd never known him to miss a chance to preach in North Elba, always about the evils of slavery. If he stood before this congregation, he'd never be able to resist striking a blow for abolition. What if someone put his face with his voice and recognized him as Osawatomie Brown? Father was jeopardizing everything he'd worked for and risked giving us all away.

I held my breath as he got up and without hesitation strode up to the pulpit. At first he talked about how he was a businessman from the north as well as a man of God. Then he brought the topic around to southern slavery, and his voice rose.

"If any man love not his brother whom he hath seen, how can he love God whom he hath not seen?" he proclaimed. "I rejoice that all the sects who bear the Christian name would have no more to do with that mother of all abominations—man-stealing."

His eyes bored into every head in the congregation. It seemed to me that anyone who before doubted the evils of human bondage could not be untouched by his forceful condemnation of it.

"The worst trial is yet to come," he went on. "God grant you thorough conversion from sin and full purpose of heart to continue steadfast in his ways through the season of tribulation you will have to pass."

He pounded his fist on the pulpit, and fire shot from his eyes. He was gristle and sinew, raw energy that seemed to come from some place beyond his thin frame, beyond the walls of the church. He called upon God, but his tarnished skin looked like it had been singed by the fires of hell. I thought of Juliet's words for Romeo when she found out he had killed her cousin Tybalt—fiend angelical, damned saint, honorable villain. They all pointed to Father. To achieve a great good, he was willing to commit a great evil. I could only wonder where it would end, and at what cost.

When Father finally finished his sermon, the large man rose to lead the last hymn, and I looked around, scanning the white faces in the church. If anyone suspected that the voice of one of slavery's most forceful opponents had just shaken the rafters, no one came forth to claim the bounty placed on John Brown's head after his Kansas exploits. I took a deep breath. We were safe for now, it seemed, but I hoped Father would not tempt fate a second time.

As we filed out of the church, some people stopped to shake Father's hand, but others turned their backs as we passed. Father's message had evidently angered as many people as it had inspired. I expected to see Mrs. Huffmaster and her brood of children, but she was not in the sanctuary. What was she up to this morning? If she paid a visit to the farm, I hoped Martha could handle her without me.

When we got back to the farm, Owen met us at the door.

"We may have some trouble, Father," he said.

Inside Oliver was comforting a tearful Martha, and Shields Green paced around the sitting room.

"What has happened?" asked Father.

"Oh, Lord, Mr. Brown," said The Emperor. "I am sorry as I can be. I didn't mean no harm." I looked around for a body, or at least some blood. What besides a killing could have him so upset?

"Calm down, now," said Father. "Just tell me what happened."

"Well, I come downstairs to see if Mrs. Brown could mend my coat." He nodded toward Martha. "I was going to offer to do some ironing for her. I'm right good at ironing."

"Yes," said Father. "And . . .?"

"That woman who been nosing around . . ."

"Mrs. Huffmaster?" I said.

"That's the one. Well, she was in the house when I come down the stairs."

"I didn't hear her come in," said Martha. She wiped her cheek with her hand.

"Did she see you?" Father asked the Emperor.

"That she did, that she did."

"Did she say anything?"

"She said, 'You a runaway?' I thought real quick. Better let her think what she was thinking than tell her anything else."

"So Mrs. Huffmaster thinks we're harboring fugitive slaves," said Father. "There may not be any harm in that."

"She may be a spy for the Federals," said Owen, at which Martha let out a cry and buried her face in Oliver's shirt.

"I wouldn't put it past them to use a farm wife as a disguise," said Oliver.

Father looked at me. "You've spoken with the woman more than any of us. Engage her in conversation and see if you can find out what she's up to. And Anna," he said, "be as polite as you can."

It was not long before Mrs. Huffmaster came around again, bringing with her a peach cobbler.

"Thought you all might like something special," she said, "in light of your company and all."

"Company?" I said.

Mrs. Huffmaster leaned toward me as if she was telling a secret. "I know you got a runaway in there. But it's none of my business. Not a single soul will hear it from Eunice Huffmaster. Don't you worry about that."

She had an excited expression on her large, good-natured face. It struck me that her happiness came not just from thinking she knew what we were up to—she also liked the idea that we were helping runaway slaves. I didn't trust her discretion with such an interesting piece of gossip, but, for now, I knew she didn't intend to give us away.

Mrs. Huffmaster didn't have the intelligence or commitment to be an active abolitionist herself, but she would bake a peach cobbler for someone who was. If she learned that Father intended to attack a United States armory and lead the slaves in rebellion, though, I had no doubt she would turn us in without hesitation. I stood at the gate long after she left, thinking about Henry Thompson's words at Timbucto: "I was with you, sir, when I thought your mission was to lead the slaves to freedom. What you have devised will end in war." Father's plan was not about freedom—it was about violence. Why had he chosen this path? Try as I might, I could not make sense of it.

Chapter 14

After the episode with Shields Green, the men were not allowed farther than the dining room during daylight hours. Late at night they could move about, but they were growing restless, and Albert Hazlett's appearance at the farm did not make matters any easier. He looked like a well-bred young man, all smiles and handshakes, and at first I thought Albert's good nature would lighten all our spirits. Little did I know that his innocent face hid an impish nature.

The strain of confinement grew worse, especially now with seventeen men in the house. Dauphin had scarcely spoken to me since he came to the farm. I looked for a wink or a nod from him—anything that would keep me from thinking I'd imagined how close we once were—but he only glanced at me when I set his plate in front of him.

One morning in early September Dauphin came to the breakfast table with a fuzzy jaw. He was usually clean-shaven, but it appeared that he hadn't taken a razor to his face for a few days. Albert ran his knuckles over Dauphin's cheek.

"Is the little boy trying to grow a beard?" Albert teased.

Dauphin knocked his hand away.

"Let's put some milk on it and get a cat to lick it off," Albert persisted.

Willy Leeman poked a finger at Dauphin's chest. "He looks more like a girl than a soldier. Maybe I can get him to darn my socks."

Dauphin stared straight ahead, his face hard as stone. I thought of Mr. Epps that day at the tannery and the way the white men taunted him. But this time it wasn't my place to step in.

"I think we've got three women among us," Albert said. "What's your name, honey? Is it Daphne?"

Dauphin was on his feet so quickly that his chair turned over behind him. He drew back a fist and glared at Albert.

"She wants to fight now," said Albert. "Maybe she'll make a soldier after all." He looked at Willy, who joined him in a good laugh.

"Hold on," said Dauphin's brother, Will, putting a hand on Dauphin's shoulder. "He's not worth skinning your knuckles for."

"Hazlett!" said Owen. "You and Leeman go up to the loft and cool off. If I hear any more mocking from either of you, you'll answer to me." His voice left no room for argument.

The two troublemakers scowled at Owen but went to the loft without another word. I felt sorry for Dauphin. He was trying so hard to be a man.

Father stared at the table, hands clenched on either side of his plate. If he didn't get the raid under way soon, the men might forget why they'd come and start a battle with each other.

"I have an idea," said Chatham. "Owen, do you have an extra sack of grain stored away?"

"Yes," said Owen. "What do you want with it?"

"If you'll haul it up to the loft, I'll show you. And bring a coil of strong rope."

Watson shouldered the fifty-pound sack and brought it upstairs, and I followed along. I was curious to see what Chatham had in mind.

He tossed an end of the rope over the rafter and tied it off so that the sack hung chest-high in the middle of the room.

"Now what?" asked Watson.

"Mr. Leeman," said Chatham, "would you like to have the first blow?"

Willy crouched in fighting position and thrust a fist at the sack. Albert took the other side, and they worked themselves into a sweat punching and jabbing at the bag.

Dangerfield Newby watched them from his cot, a creased letter unfolded on his knee.

"Annie," he said, "you think you can find me a clean sheet of paper?"

"There's some paper in Father's desk," I said. "Are you writing to your wife?"

"Listen to what she says here. 'You are my one bright hope. Come as soon as you can. Oh, that blessed hour when I shall see you again.' Now, ain't my Harriet something?" A wide grin slit his thin face nearly in half. "I'm going to get her out of slavery or die trying."

"I'll get you that paper," I said. I didn't want to hear about dying.

Just as I got to the stairs, I heard a loud thud followed by a stream of curses. I turned around and saw Albert and Willy standing by the broken sack, their feet buried in pearly grains of barley.

Dangerfield slowly folded his wife's letter and slipped it into the pocket of his vest, where he always kept it.

Maybe it was because of the tension in the house that I was sleeping lightly at night. A noise outside my bedroom window brought me upright in bed. Pistol in hand, I looked outside. Two figures were making their way away from the house, through the pasture and into the woods— two figures that looked very much like Willy Leeman and Albert Hazlett. They must have shinnied down a rope from the upstairs window.

I tried to stay awake until they came back, but I must have dozed off. It was just getting light when I heard Father's voice in the front room.

"Just where have you two been?" he asked.

"Gone for a walk, old man," said Willy. "Couldn't sleep."

"A walk where?" said Father.

"Not far," said Albert. "We didn't encounter any hostile parties."

"Wandering around in the middle of the night is not a lark, men," Father said. "If you're found out, you'll jeopardize our entire operation. Now, where were you?"

Someone coughed. Then Albert spoke.

"We went to Harpers Ferry, if you must know. Visited with John Cook and his wife. No harm done." He slurred his words, and I wouldn't have been surprised if he'd had a few ales.

Someone was pacing the floor—I assumed it was Father

because I heard his voice next.

"You seem to have forgotten the reason we're here, the reason you signed up with me. If you're questioning our purpose, then you're free to leave—but do so now."

I waited for an answer, but I heard nothing.

"If you choose to renew your commitment to our plan," Father continued, "you will do so under my conditions. First, you are not to leave this house again, under any circumstances. Second, you will come down from the loft only at mealtimes. Third, there will be no drinking nor smoking as long as you're under my command. Is that clear?"

"Yes, sir," said Albert.

"Leeman?" said Father.

A long pause.

"All right, old man," he said at last.

Even after getting a good tongue-lashing, I could tell by the rudeness in Willy's voice that his mischief wasn't over.

Chapter 15

The next few days were thankfully quiet. I didn't see Albert or Willy except for breakfast and supper, and then they were both sullen and went back to the loft as soon as they'd eaten. They eased up on tormenting Dauphin, too, much to my relief.

One morning after breakfast Father rode into Harpers Ferry with Owen and Watson to look around. Oliver kept a lookout on the porch with Martha, and Dauphin helped me carry the dishes downstairs to the sink. While I washed, he scraped a fingernail with the edge of his knife.

"Annie," he said, "the raid has to happen soon."

"What makes you say that, Dauphin?" I asked.

"The men can't take much more waiting. They're itching for action—it's all they talk about."

"Don't they think that Father knows what he's doing?" I no longer believed in Father's plan myself. My dread wouldn't go away.

"Some of the men are beginning to doubt that he does."

I stopped washing and wiped my hands on my apron. "And you, Dauphin? Are you having second thoughts about the raid?"

He folded his knife and looked at me. He was always so shy that he'd only give me a quick glance, but now he stared into my eyes.

"I'm not afraid to die," he said. "Except for one thing."

"And what is that, Dauphin?" I studied his face, the face I knew so well—his pale lashes and sky-blue eyes, his peachy skin and soft lips. I would never tire of looking at him.

"I always hoped that one day . . ." He wet his lips with his tongue and took a deep breath. "There have already been two weddings between the Thompsons and the Browns . . ."

"That's true." I knew what he was trying to say, but I wanted to hear it anyway.

"So, it seems natural that you and I . . ."

I tried to push the raid from my mind, but I couldn't. It was the reason we were standing here, the reason we might never marry, as Dauphin was proposing. He was right to have second thoughts about the attack. What I had seen, what I had felt—it all added up to one thing. Death. Father would be sending Martha and me back to North Elba soon, maybe even within the next few days. I didn't have much time.

"Dauphin," I said, "come back with me."

"What do you mean?" he said.

"Father will never let Martha and me stay for the attack. Leave with us."

"You're asking me to quit? To abandon the rest of the men?"

"I'm asking you to save your life. I know what's going to happen. I've seen things." I wanted to go on and tell him about the visions, but I stopped. He would never believe me.

"Annie," he said, "I'm not the bravest man in the world, but I'm no coward. No matter what happens, I've got to see this through." He put his hands on my shoulders.

"Wait for me," he said. "We're meant to be together."

Hard as I tried, I couldn't conjure up an image of Dauphin and me as husband and wife, farming, raising a family. I thought of Romeo and Juliet; they knew their love was heading straight toward doom. When Juliet said on the balcony, "I have no joy in this contract—it is too rash, too ill-advis'd, too sudden, too like lightning," she might as well have been talking about the assault on Harpers Ferry. The two lovers brought peace to Verona, but they paid for it with their lives. The end of slavery would cost the same price. Father was the only one who could call off the raid, but I didn't think he could be deterred, even by the doubts of his men. There was nothing to do but go on.

"I would like to be your wife one day, Dauphin," I said truthfully, but my heart was breaking.

When he kissed me and I breathed in his sweet hay smell, it was autumn and not spring that I saw. Hard as I wished with all my heart that it could be a beginning, I knew it was an ending.

The men had just returned from town when dark clouds moved in so that it looked like dusk rather than high noon. Father went to his desk and worked over his maps and figures while flashes of lightning struck around us, and explosions of thunder shook the floorboards. Rain pelted

96

down on the roof. Tree branches beat against the house, and wet leaves pressed themselves onto the windows.

Some of the men came down from the loft to look out at the storm. Albert began to jump up and down every time the thunder sounded, and then Willy bounced next to him. At the next clap, Dangerfield Newby and Shields Green began to dance about, and soon Dauphin and the others leaped and yelled with each thunderclap. They ran up and down the stairs whooping and screaming like wild men. The storm drowned out the sound of their uproar for nearly half an hour, long enough for the men to let off some steam. Father must have approved because he kept his nose in his books the whole time and never said a word.

The storm was the crest of the wave leading up to the attack. After the thunder died away and the rain stopped, the men fell into a quiet that was unsettling, as if each was preparing himself for what was about to happen.

When John Cook came from Harpers Ferry with satchel in hand, I knew the time was getting close. He brought another man with him, handsome and well-groomed, twenty years or so younger than Father with an intelligent look in his soft eyes. I liked him immediately.

"Annie," said Father, "this is John Kagi, my secretary of war. Should anything happen to me, the men will answer to him."

Should anything happen to Father . . .

I saw Father lying wounded, surrounded by uniformed men, weak and near death. Limp bodies lay about him. Blood formed puddles on the ground. I recognized John Kagi, Stewart Taylor, Jeremiah Anderson . . . and three other men whose faces were distorted in death. I smelled gunpowder. I heard yelling, wood splintering, glass breaking. I tried to swallow, but my throat was too dry.

Light glinted from Father's saber leaning against a corner, and I focused on it to dispel the vision. Did I imagine it, or was the blade smeared with red? No! Please let it stop! I thought I was shouting, but my cry must only have echoed in my head. Father went on as if nothing had happened.

"Mr. Kagi came to Kansas to report stories for newspapers," said Father. "He got involved in the fighting, though, and proved himself a warrior."

I forced myself to come back to my senses.

"Until I was arrested," said Mr. Kagi. "I wasn't much use those four months I spent in jail."

"The proslavery judiciary in Kansas was a mockery," said Father. "The case never should have gone to court."

"The judge and I had a little shoot-out," said Mr. Kagi.

"Shoot-out? In court?" I said and sat down to steady myself.

"The judge struck Mr. Kagi over the head with his gold-handled cane," said Father.

"Smartly enough to open a gash in my skull. I drew my revolver and shot him in the thigh, although I might have done better to aim a little higher."

"You shot the judge?" I asked. I didn't think I'd heard him right.

"The judge retaliated by drawing his own gun, and he shot Kagi over the heart," said Father.

"And you survived?" I said.

"Fortunately," Mr. Kagi laughed, "I had a memorandum book in my pocket, which stopped the slug. And the case was thrown out."

Had the whole country gone crazy? If the battle over slavery had found its way into the courtrooms, where would the violence stop?

While Martha sat her watch on the front porch, I swept the dining room, listening to the muffled talk of the men in the loft. Father stared at his work, shuffling papers and tapping his pen on the desk. Finally he got up.

"Anna," he said, "you and Martha keep an eye out. I'm going up to meet with the men." Something was wrong— I could sense it.

I sat on the middle step leading to the loft so that if Martha saw anyone, she would call to me, and I would alert Father. From where I sat, my pistol on my lap, I could see the men sitting on their bedrolls, propped on an elbow or leaning against the wall. Dauphin sat with his elbows on his knees and stared at his hands, fingers laced together. Father stood with his foot on the rung of a chair, his hand rubbing his knee. His white beard billowed about his face like a cloud of breath on a frosty North Elba morning. For him, I knew nothing existed but the group of conspirators surrounding him—the conspirators and the plan.

"Men," Father said, "a young black man died last week. Why did he die? His wife was sold to another plantation. At the thought of never seeing her again, he hanged himself." One arm was stiff at his side, a batch of papers in his hand. His gray eyes flashed from one man to another.

"We are too late to bring him back to life," Father continued, "but we may be able to prevent more deaths like his. As you know, I had intended to wait until spring to launch our attack. But circumstances favor earlier action, likely the middle of October."

My heart rose in my throat. That was just a few weeks from now. I looked at my father's wiry body, muscle and nerve holding his frail form together. Was he an angel sent to free the black man or a demon who would turn the country upside down? He was my father, but only by blood. I couldn't remember being held on his knee, and he was rarely there on birthdays or holidays. Being his child meant obedience, loyalty, patience, strength. But this was his most challenging battle, and he had trained his children to be his soldiers. Owen, Watson, Oliver—and Dauphin—would follow him and fight for him. And no matter what I thought about him and his plan, I dared not speak out against him in front of the men.

"Virginia has fifty-eight thousand free Negroes and almost half a million slaves," said Father. "More blacks than any other Southern state. The sentiment for rebellion will be on our side. But we desperately need more arms for our mission." He raised the papers over his head.

"I've mapped out our plan, and I want you all to listen closely. We'll attack Harpers Ferry and capture the government armory and arsenal, including the rifle works. Maryland and Virginia are full of people like us who oppose slavery, and once we have weapons, we'll take control of the town and hold out until they join us. When the attack begins, word will spread quickly and slaves will drop their work and bolt from the plantations to take up arms against their oppressors."

Father stopped again—perhaps too long. The men were silent until Mr. Tidd spoke.

"Just a minute," he said. "I joined this venture thinking we would set slaves free, as we did in Missouri. I had no idea you planned to overthrow the entire Federal government. I smell treason, sir."

"You're right, Tidd," said Father. "The purpose of our army is to rescue slaves. Those who don't want to fight will be led north into Canada. We'll move south and liberate slaves and take hostages. Once we have Virginia, the slaves in the Southern states will fight for themselves. Meanwhile, we'll raid more arsenals and drive into Tennessee, Alabama, Mississippi, Georgia, the Carolinas. There are nearly two million blacks in the Southern states—we cannot fail to rouse them."

"I'm against it," protested Mr. Tidd. He stood up from his cot. "It's suicide for a handful of men to try to take a whole town. We'll be battling Federal troops, trained men." He took a step forward, but Father's voice stopped him.

"Mr. Tidd," said Father, "do you remember the soldiers in Kansas? They were a lazy, drunken lot. I think we'll encounter little trouble."

Oliver spoke next. "I've been scouting Harpers Ferry," he said. "The rivers are too swift to swim across, and the mountain behind the town will make it impossible to escape. I'm afraid we might be trapped in the armory."

"Escape is not part of the plan," said Father. "We're here to fight."

"I've studied the layout of the government buildings," said Mr. Cook. He was sitting on a hardback chair, one leg crossed over the other. He seemed relaxed even when he was talking about revolution. "The watchmen are complacent. They spend most of their time playing cards or dozing off, and a forcible capture would take them unawares. I'm for attacking at once."

"I'm in agreement," said Jeremiah Anderson.

Shields Green spoke. "I been cut by the overseer's lash. It bit into my back and it bit into my soul. If the plan frees my people, I'm ready to lay down my life with old Mr. Brown."

"I'm with the Emperor," said Dangerfield Newby. He must have been thinking of Harriet and his children.

"If we move quickly," said Mr. Kagi, "we can take the Ferry by surprise and then slip into the mountains. That way we'll avoid being captured, and we can set up the mountain state we've talked about."

"I'll go along with you," said Stewart Taylor. He looked at the floor and shook his head. "But I know one thing—I'll be the first to die."

"Nonsense," said Willy Leeman. "We'll outnumber them by the time the blacks from all around join us."

"What makes you so sure they'll join?" Mr. Tidd asked.

Father answered for him. "The attack will be a trumpet to rally them. They'll know that their friends have come."

"None of us will get out alive," said Tidd. "And even if a few do, they'll be taken and hanged."

"Tidd may be right," said Oliver. He looked worried. Maybe he was thinking of Martha; she was too young to be a widow.

"Of course I'm right," said Tidd.

The men argued in loud voices, and I strained my neck to see Martha on the porch. If Mrs. Huffmaster came along now, she would surely hear them. They must have forgotten what danger they were in—or maybe they realized that the peril of being found in the farmhouse was nothing compared to what they would face in the next month.

Finally the debate died down, and Father took in a slow breath and spoke.

"If you feel so strongly, perhaps it is better that I resign as commander-in-chief," he said.

My heart thumped in my chest. He couldn't be giving up. He wouldn't turn his back on what he'd believed in so strongly. I had to believe his resignation was a bluff.

Father came past me down the stairs to his desk and sat still as stone, leaning his forehead on his palms. I ran my hand over the pine board of the step. It was worn smooth in the middle but rough on the sides, and a splinter dug into my skin. When I pulled the tiny wooden spike out with my teeth, a drop of blood oozed out.

Voices drifted down from the loft, so soft I couldn't make out what they said. I needed a breath of air and wandered out to where Martha sat guard on the porch.

"What do you think's happening?" she asked.

"I don't know," I said. "But some of the men are questioning the wisdom of the raid, and Father just offered to resign."

"What? They can't give up now." Martha was almost pleading.

"Martha, I . . ." I paused, wondering how I should put my fears into words. "I have a bad feeling about the raid. I think they could all be killed," I said.

"Annie, I don't want to have a baby in a country that allows innocent people to be held prisoners. Don't you remember the man we helped on the way to the farm? The one on the wagon? I never want my child to know that kind of cruelty."

"Even if it means Oliver could die trying to stop it?"

Martha put a hand on her stomach. Her eyes filled with tears, but her head was high. "I would be proud to know my husband died for such a worthy cause," she said.

No matter how I tried, I couldn't be so selfless as my sister-in-law. I wanted to feel proud about what my father and brothers were trying to do, but all I felt were fear and sadness.

I went back inside and stood at Father's desk. His fingers were pressed to his temples, and he looked to be deep in thought. But he was alone, and I could be silent no longer.

"Call it off," I said.

Father's brows drew together as if he hadn't understood what I'd said.

"Call off the raid," I repeated, heart pounding, avoiding his stare.

"Did you not hear me offer my resignation?" he asked.

"I don't believe a word of it." I was on dangerous ground. All my life I'd been taught not to talk back to my elders, especially to my parents. Now I was speaking to Father as if I were his equal. I knew he would not approve of my lack of humility, but I could think of no better way to get his attention.

"My strange Anna," he said. His smile made me furious. The lives of the men I loved were at stake, and he was treating me as a little girl.

"It's senseless to follow through with your plan," I said, and this time I looked into his eyes so that he would see the conviction in mine.

He heaved a long, tired sigh. I suppose he didn't expect such lack of faith or such a direct criticism from me. "Eighty years ago, our forefathers battled for America's freedom from England," he said. "To be a subject of the king was to be a slave, they believed. This country was founded on liberty and justice for all. To enslave any of its members is hypocrisy and treason. If I don't fight for the freedom of every individual, I will be a hypocrite and a traitor. Worst of all, my inaction will allow slavery to continue." He looked straight back at me.

I remembered the alarm I felt that day in North Elba when Father and I stood by the big rock. "If my path leads into the valley of death," he had said, "I know that

God intends some good to come of it." Alarm rushed through me again as I realized why Father's plan did not include retreat if things went badly. He was preparing to march into that valley. And he knew he was probably leading his sheep there as well.

"Your action will kill innocent people." My voice was firm. I wouldn't let it quaver. "You will sacrifice my brothers, Dauphin, everyone. It's not worth it. It's madness."

We had been speaking low, but Father dropped his voice still more.

"If that is what you believe," he said in an icy tone, "you are no daughter of John Brown."

His glare pierced me, and I thought of the stag on Whiteface Mountain, pinned to the ledge, unable to move. I now knew what it felt like to oppose my father. His will, his zeal overwhelmed me. I struggled to counter it, but no words would come out of my open mouth. All I could see were Father's eyes, cold as steel.

Owen cleared his throat. I hadn't heard him come down the stairs, but now he stood beside me. He looked at us for a moment before speaking.

"The men have all agreed to abide by your decisions," he said to Father, "and we're willing to pay whatever price it takes. As for Oliver and Watson and me—if our father goes to his death, he will not go alone."

Father's ploy had worked. Mutiny had been avoided, and now only the final designs were left to be added to the plan. I felt exhausted and beaten. There was nothing more for me to do but ask God to help John Brown and his men.

Chapter 16

———

The end of September was near. I had gotten to know the men as brothers, and I knew I would miss them. But none of us could go on like this much longer. In North Elba the leaves would be changing color and the northern cold would be leaving its white trail of frost on the fields at night. I thought about Mother and Sarah and Ellen, and I wished again we could all go home. But the men would stay, and soon they would fight.

Before we left, Martha and I cleaned the house and put the kitchen in order so the men could cook their own meals when we were gone. Then we harvested the garden and stored the vegetables in the root cellar. I thought about Mrs. Huffmaster every now and then, but since seeing Shields Green, she had contented herself with waving from the gate when she passed by.

The night before Martha and I were to leave, Father came into my room while I was packing. He had spoken little to me since our argument.

"Take these back to your mother," he said, holding out the lace doilies she had sent down with us. "She'll want to keep them." His hands were rough—shooting hands, killing hands, hands too coarse to be holding such delicate things.

I took them and laid them on top of my clothes. "Will you want the gun back, Father?" I asked.

"Keep it," he said. "You never know when you'll be called to use it." Most of my life I had known my father to be a peace-loving man. He never believed in hunting or fishing, but in growing his own food by the sweat of his brow. When he killed his livestock, it was only to feed his family. Now his weapons were as much a part of him as his arms and legs—and he was asking that I make them part of me.

"I'll keep it for protection," I said, "but I pray that I'll never fire it again."

Father left the room without saying another word.

The morning of our departure, we made a large breakfast for the men and got our bags ready to load onto the wagon. Money had run so low that we couldn't afford train fare, so Oliver would drive us back to North Elba and then return alone.

As we stood at the door to say our good-byes, Shields Green stepped forward, rubbed his forehead with one hand, and shifted his weight from one foot to the other.

"You gracious women done your utmost for us," he said, "and it's with highest heartfelt that we see you go."

The Emperor didn't have much education, but he was speaking from his heart, which was more touching than the most eloquent speech. I looked around the rickety old farmhouse for the last time, at the decrepit furniture and the scratched floors. I would not miss them, but I would miss the men. I looked at them to remember their faces—Albert Hazlett, Willy Leeman, Dangerfield Newby, and all the rest. Finally, my gaze fell on Dauphin.

He stepped forward, a bundle under his arm.

"Take care of this for me, Annie. I'll get it when I come home." It was his pillow—he'd have no soft place to lay his head. I took it and held it close to me.

Then, as all the men were watching, he took my hand briefly, squeezed it, and stepped back among the others like a soldier falling into line. I held my head up, determined to keep my departure dignified. Even though a sob sounded somewhere deep down inside, I did not let it surface to betray me.

Father walked us to the wagon and kissed my cheek. It was a peace offering that I could not bring myself to return. As Oliver drove down the rutted driveway, past the shed filled with weapons that would be called into action soon, I patted Father's pistol tucked into the waistband of my skirt and looked back at the Kennedy farm. Father stood at the gate, thin as a spear, with the men a blur behind him.

As I turned away from him, the farmhouse, and the men, I thought of Dauphin, standing tall, so dear . . . I pressed my face to his pillow and breathed him in for the last time, and the tears I had battled for so long finally defeated me.

Chapter 17

Autumn was a valiant time of year in North Elba. The leaves were afire with red and orange, and the sun shimmered on the bare rock at the top of Whiteface Mountain. The bright colors were the last gasp of nature's life before sinking into winter's deathly slumber. I'd never felt so melancholy.

One Sunday in October we went to church as usual—Mother walking with Belle and Martha, Abbie on Salmon's arm, Sarah, Ellen and I following behind. The sermon didn't stir me. It was about Sodom and Gomorrah and Lot's wife turning to a pillar of salt when she looked back at the burning cities. I wanted to look forward. I wanted to imagine a future of peace and happiness, a future with all my family together again. But my dreams wouldn't let me.

That night I had the worst nightmare yet. I was back at Harpers Ferry, at the engine house. I saw smoke and fire and violence and confusion. Lead exploded from rifles. Steel blades flashed. My ears rang with angry shouts, pounding heartbeats, dying gasps.

Then, finally, through the smoke and the chaos I saw men. Men I knew. And what was happening to them was beyond any horror I had ever imagined.

Dangerfield Newby fell, his hand over his vest pocket, over his wife's letter, shot through the chest. His body rolled into a ditch.

Shots caught John Kagi in the shoulder, the stomach. His body went limp, his eyes staring into black space.

Will Thompson waved a white flag, his face showing all was lost. The flag did him no good—a lead ball shot through his skull. Men flung his body into the river, took aim, and shot him again and again, their rage not satisfied by his death.

Willy Leeman had no flag, but he raised his hands in surrender. A gun pointed close at his face. A single shot rang out, and his angelic face was a hideous mess of blood.

Bodies lay scattered over the floor of the engine house. Stewart Taylor. Jeremiah Anderson. Watson. Oliver. Under a fire engine, Dauphin, my beloved Dauphin, lay still. His face was untouched, and he seemed at peace. My wild hope lasted an instant, but then I saw blood and the wound where a saber had pierced his heart.

And Father. Beaten and bloodied, he had fallen in the middle of the floor. I couldn't see him clearly behind the feet of the uniformed men who swarmed everywhere. I did not know if he, too, was dead.

I woke shaking. It was cold, so cold, and for a moment I didn't know who or where I was. Then I came fully awake and staggered outside in the blackness, trying

110

to fight down the sickness I felt. I gulped in the frosty air, my breath billowing out in clouds of steam. I had just seen the raid. The army's opposition had been overwhelming and vicious. John Brown and his men had failed.

I had had enough. I wanted no more dreams, no more visions.

The next day I wandered around in a fog, feeding the chickens, gathering eggs, and bringing in firewood without any feeling, just going through the motions. In my heart I was still by the Shenendoah River, living Father's last battle against slavery.

When I came downstairs Tuesday morning, Mr. Hinkley stood in the parlor, looking out the window. I knew at once why he was there. Mother was rocking Ellen, and Sarah and Martha were by her side. Salmon, in the middle of the room, held a newspaper.

No one said a word when I came in; no one moved. Finally Mr. Hinkley pulled a handkerchief out of his pocket and coughed into it.

"What is it?" I asked.

"Annie, sit down," Salmon said.

"No, I won't sit down," I said. "It's about Harpers Ferry, isn't it?"

Salmon heaved a deep sigh and dropped his arms so that the paper dangled from one hand.

"They held the raid Sunday night," he said. "The raiders took prisoners—slaveowners and a colonel—and set up in the engine house. By daybreak the military moved in and the fighting began."

The shooting echoed in my mind. "They're dead, aren't they?" I said.

"Owen, Barclay Coppoc, Hazlett, Cook, Tidd,

111

Chatham Anderson—they all escaped. Forces captured Edwin Coppoc, Aaron Stevens, and Shields Green, and they're in prison. Father was stabbed and beaten, but he's alive. They have him under armed guard until they can arrange his trial."

"The rest?" I said.

Salmon shook his head.

I was numb, too numb to cry. Weeping and wailing wouldn't have expressed what I felt anyway. Nothing could.

In the days that followed, we read newspaper accounts of what happened after the raid. The courts wasted no time in having Father's trial. Angry mobs tried to lynch him in Harpers Ferry, so he was moved to a prison in Charlestown. Because of his injuries, he had to be carried into the courtroom on a cot, but he raised up on an elbow to answer questions that lawyers hurled at him for hour upon hour. The slaves had not lost an advocate. Father spoke their cause as long as there were ears to listen.

Even so, the jury took only forty-five minutes to find him guilty. Treason against Virginia, conspiring to lead a slave rebellion, murder in the first degree. On the last day of November, he would face the gallows. I had seen it coming, but that was no comfort to me now.

Lyman Epps came with a letter from town. I met him at the door and took the envelope. It was addressed to Martha. I ran my finger over her name. "Martha B. Brown, Timbucto, North Elba, New York." It was Oliver's handwriting, probably written just before the raid.

In the dining room, Martha had quilt pieces strewn across the table top. She was quilting a blanket for the baby, due in just a few more months. When I handed her the letter, she tore it open.

"Listen, Annie," she said. "Oliver says, 'You can hardly think how lonesome it was the day I left you, but if I can do a single good action, my life will not have been all a failure.'" Then she smiled serenely, as if it would not be long before she saw him again. How could she be so brave?

"Martha?" I said softly. She was lost in the letter. "Martha, did you ever tell Oliver about the baby?"

She turned her head from side to side. No. If he had known, he might not have gone back to Harpers Ferry. He might have lived to see his child.

I walked across the barren field. Someone should have plowed it under for the winter, but who was there to do it? Salmon had all he could handle as the only man on the farm. The hillsides were stark and gray, the leaves fallen from the branches, and snow already covered the tops of Mt. Marcy and Whiteface. It would be a long, long winter.

I thought about the broad fields in Virginia, the fertile countryside with tall stalks of corn, the white farmhouses and soft mounds of the Blue Ridge Mountains rising up beyond them, all bathed in a warm blue haze. It was beautiful country, although I hadn't thought about it then.

In the distance I heard the faint tolling of the church bell. Strange for it to ring on Friday morning. I could not know, but I did know, that at that moment my father's body was hanging from a rope, his soul suspended between heaven and hell. John Brown was dead.

I turned toward the great stone where Father would be laid to rest. Frozen crystals of ice clung to it and glistened in the waning light. The stone grew wider as it met the ground, as if it were the tip of a buried mountain rising from the center of the earth. I touched the cold, hard surface and looked at the leaden sky. A flock of geese flew over, squawking and flapping in a vee formation, and all around me snowflakes floated down like soft white feathers.

Epilogue

The old lady turned the pages of the book on her lap until she came to the end of the story. "A glooming peace this morning with it brings," it read. Yes, there had been peace, after many lives were lost, after the country was torn apart. Her father had done his job better than he ever knew; he had incited the war that purged the land of its greatest evil.

When she turned the last page, a folded paper fell to the floor. Slowly she bent and picked it up with her frail fingers. It was a letter dated November 30, 1859. A letter from her father. It had been a long time since Annie Brown had read those words, a long time since she had stood at the foot of the mountain in northern New York with the outline of a white stag etched on its side. The images washed over her again, fresh and clear as that autumn day so many years ago.

"I am awaiting the hour of my public murder with

great composure and cheerfulness," her father wrote. "So my dear shattered and broken family, be of good cheer and believe and trust in God with all your heart. I never felt stronger confidence in the certain and near approach of a bright morning and a glorious day."

Annie folded the letter and slipped it back into the book. She placed it again in the bottom of the trunk, along with the old pistol, Dauphin's pillow, the quilts and the doilies, and closed the lid. She looked at the sun coming through the attic window. It was indeed a bright morning. She had made peace with her father's memory, and for the first time in many, many years, it would be a glorious day.